WHY YOU NEED TO READ THIS BOOK!

I choked up at a wedding the other day, but for a reason you might not guess. It was sad for me to see my buddy Tim Mauricio sitting on the front row at his son Dallas' wedding and knowing that he's not hearing one word, one sound. But that doesn't stop Tim. In fact, I laughed when he told me about going to see Van Halen with Dallas, and from their seat close to the stage, Tim yelled this question into Dallas' ear, *"Have they played 'Jump' yet?"* And Dallas responded, "Yeah, they're playing it right now!"

Watch a day of TV with the sound on mute and see what you get out of it; see how involved you are in what's going on, and see how long you can stand it before you either lose interest or put the sound back on. And you can't use closed-captioning because life doesn't have subtitles.

Tim can't turn the sound back on in the world he lives now. He can't sit around the campfire anymore and stare into the glow, listening to what people say. He can't walk into a party and decide which conversation he'd like to be a part of. He's a master at reading lips, and one-on-one he does well. But he depends on others to give him that attention, and we don't always do that.

As you'll discover, he lost more than his hearing. He lost his balance, the ability to focus his eyes, his career, and social ease. But he didn't lose his spirit, and he tells this amazing story in the pages of this book. It's great story! Yes it's sad, but it's also a story of adapting and fighting through each day to win another battle, even though he knows that the struggle will never be done. I'm glad Tim wrote this book, and I hope you find it as compelling as I did. It's a real story, a story of how life happens to all of us and of how Tim Mauricio overcame.

Bob Taylor
Co-Founder,
President
Taylor Guitars

To Milton and Eunice,

SOUND-CHECK

A JOURNEY FROM DEAF TO LIFE

May you be blessed as you read my testimony of God's unfailing love.

TIMOTHY SCOTT MAURICIO

Dedication

With deepest love and gratitude to my loving wife Monica

Thank you for your constant love, support, and belief in me. This life's journey of mine has not been easy for you, and yet your faithfulness has never diminished or faltered. You are an amazing woman, and your godly influence upon my life is one which continually inspires me to love and honor God in all that I do.

To Dallas and Brittney

No father could ever be more proud of his children than I am of you!

Acknowledgement

A special thanks to Cindy Taylor

More than being my editor, you are a most treasured blessing as a friend and encourager. Thank you for your wisdom and discernment, which allowed this book to come to fruition as you continually shared your ideas and motivated me to tell my story.

Contents

Foreword xiii
Prelude xvii
1. Developing The Song List 1
2. Beginnings 5
3. The Rhythm of the Night 9
4. My Old School 11
5. Who Let the Dogs Out? 15
6. Urgent 18
7. Monophobia 22
8. Yakety Yak 26
9. Rockin' Down the Highway 30
10. Message in a Bottle 33
11. Weird Science 36
12. Double Vision 40
13. Soul Vaccination 43
14. Hold on for One More Day 46
15. Hold on Loosely 50
16. Walk This Way 53
17. I Love Music 56
18. Dizzy… My Head is Spinning 59
19. Communication Breakdown 62

20. We Can Work It Out ... 67
21. Stairway to Heaven or a Highway to Hell ... 72
22. Lessons in Love ... 79
23. So Much More in Love ... 82
24. Enjoy the Silence ... 88
25. Silent Night ... 92
26. Friends ... 94
27. Patiently ... 100
28. Don't Stop Believin' ... 104
29. Will It Go Round in Circles? ... 109
30. Purple Haze ... 115
31. Ain't No Mountain High Enough ... 119
32. Prayer for You ... 124
Afterword: Timothy's Mission ... 127

Foreword

I simply can't say enough about Tim Mauricio. In fact, it would take another book to try to describe the sincerity and character of this man, from one who's looked on from the outside and observed the love and friendship of such a person. It would be ambiguous to say that Tim has total hearing loss, because so many times he has sent messages to me by e-mail asking how he can pray for me and it would be exactly at the time I needed a brother to agree with me in prayer. Oh yes, Tim can still hear, but in a way that so many people can't.

In 2004, I went through a very similar experience as Tim, but only on the right side of my head. It is commonly called an "acoustic neuroma," a tumor that attaches itself to the nerve connecting the ear to the brain. The approach I chose for the removal is also considered brain surgery. I remember waking up in the hospital room and everything was just spinning around, and I would get very sick in a matter of moments. Because this part of the brain is where the balance nerve lies, I had complete vertigo after the nerve was severed. The good news was that I had another balance nerve that would eventually compensate for the loss of the one from my right side. I basically had to learn to walk again. Just riding in a car and going over a speed bump was like riding on Space Mountain at Disney World, but not nearly as fun. Tim had already gone through this before me.

In my own experience, I had terrible headaches for three years, making a normal migraine "a walk in the park." Besides that, I lost total hearing on my right side, which is the very thing I had tried to avoid. I had chosen to take the more difficult approach to remove the tumor surgically and thereby try to save my hearing. Tim was there constantly encouraging me by e-mail. Again, Tim had already gone through this before me.

Bob Taylor of Taylor Guitars is a longtime friend of Tim and mine. Bob had told me of his good friend and fellow worship team drummer, Tim Mauricio, and how he had a genetic disease that would soon totally take his hearing. He also told me that Tim was the best drummer he had ever had the privilege of working with. He described how he played with such feeling and was so "musical" in his playing. Bob tried to give me perspective by explaining that my situation, as bad as it was, was nowhere near what his friend Tim had gone through and was still facing. Tim was familiar with the headaches, vertigo, and loss of hearing but Bob shared how Tim was going to have to go through the same surgery again, as he had another tumor on the other side and, without a complete miracle, would lose all his hearing.

Bob tried to explain that you can't just block out hearing by plugging your ears, because you "can still hear"! It's true. You can try to block outside sounds with other noises, plug your ears, or dive into the ocean, but you can still hear your own voice and other sounds inside your head. Being deaf on one side isn't like being "half-deaf." I can still hear! Total deafness is total silence except for the incredible "roaring" sound that is unaffected by outside sounds since it is, in fact, "all in your head." I have that roaring sound in my right ear, but Tim has that, and only that, roaring in his head twenty-four hours a day. The beautiful thing is he can hear *past* that and sense God speaking to his heart, and he listens and responds. So, I guess you could say that Tim is not totally deaf but hears what most hearing people can't. Sometimes I think we're too busy, selfish, or so attached to our physical hearing that we tend to ignore our ability to hear from God in our "inner ear" or spirit. No doubt Tim learned this before he lost his physical hearing since he was a believer in Christ and a student of the Word.

Tim remembers sounds. He can still stand, look you in the eyes, and speak as though everything were normal, and unless you knew, you just wouldn't know that he can't hear a thing you're saying or even what he himself is saying! He can read your lips, your emotions, and can sense things.

He sensed that someone needed to read his story. Perhaps he sensed that his words would dig under your pain and pull out a nugget of hope and courage to help get you through the situation that has come your way right now. Tim inherited a problem and circumstances that he didn't deserve. Yet Tim deserves to be heard, and I assure you he would say that God deserves all the credit for his testimony. Tim and I both agree that bad circumstances don't have to make you want to pull away from God and be bitter. On the contrary, although dealing with trials in life is a battle and we have questions sometimes, our faith says we "know" in our "knower" that God deeply cares and understands, and that He loves us with an "unchanging love" and knows what is best for our lives. This book is all about that. It's about love and family and how we can indeed overcome any obstacle, and how faith, forgiveness, and walking in love is a language that God Himself hears. This is a book that speaks to you from the inside out! It's about how we're never alone. God is always there ... always!

Although I've tried to explain my past experiences a bit, this book is not about me or my life. I am merely trying to give you a glimpse of who Tim really is and how he's such an overcomer. As a guitar player, I often play in churches with the deaf sections off to the side and see their interpreters signing and sometimes giving them a balloon so they can feel the vibrations of my music. Sometimes I feel unworthy to stand in their presence. I see their love for the Lord on their faces. I sense their hunger to know more and receive more of God.

Take time to look around and try to understand that the hunger inside of us to know God goes beyond our human senses or their failures and flaws. This hunger can only be satisfied by the Lord Jesus Christ who also didn't deserve His suffering, but did it all for you and me. I'll never forget how, after my surgery, Tim wrote and asked if I had regained my hearing on my right side. When I explained that I had not, he said that if he could, he would gladly give up his good side so that I could hear in both my ears. He meant it, too. Not long after that, Tim went into his silent world. Let's go into his world and see the truth of Psalm 139:7: "Where can I go from Your Spirit? Or where can I flee from Your Presence?" That is what this book is about.

Doyle Dykes
Family man, musician, minister, and author

Prelude

I write these words after having completed the writing of my story. After months of reflection, I've come to realize that there are a multitude of directions one can take when writing his biography or life's story. That is, some personal experiences can be greatly embellished or diminished depending on the heights or depths the authors are willing to bare their souls to their readers.

In putting my story to paper, I wrote many of the pages with overwhelming emotions. Some of these pages came with great sadness and weeping while recalling the pain of those specific time periods. Additionally, other periods of writing were filled with tears of joy as I contemplated the vast blessings I'm most grateful for in life.

After numerous revisions, I can tell you unequivocally that my utmost desire and paramount concern is that the ensuing words will bring forth hope, encouragement, and blessings in your life.

What I'm most compelled to communicate from the very onset is that without God being in my life, I'd have no story worth writing and no testimony to reveal. It is therefore that I solely endeavor to put my journey into written word, for the *soul* purpose (the purpose of the soul) and to bear witness to God's faithfulness and for His glory alone.

Developing The Song List

Some days are easier than others, yet not a single day has passed when I haven't missed the sounds of life. As a former professional musician for over twenty years, I can tell you that the sounds of silence are nothing to hum about. Going from a world where sound was everything to me, becoming totally deaf and trying to adapt to the ongoing challenges is more than just an adventure; it's an entirely different world. It is a more formidable mountain than I'd ever imagined facing yet one I'm committed to climbing.

What you are about to read encompasses a span of over fifteen years. This journey has been filled with great blessings and joy, but also significant emotional pain, physical suffering, and the daily challenges of enduring multiple permanent disabilities incurred from having an extremely rare genetic disorder.

As you'll discover, music was a huge part of my world for the better part of my life. Since it was one of my greatest loves, I've chosen (embracing a more thematic approach) to name the chapters of my journey after various song titles.

Some write their story in chronological order, going from point A to point B. And although some of my writing is done in a similar fashion, I chose to convey many of the most significant aspects of my story thematically in hopes of inspiring you to pause and reflect on those things in life which we so often take for granted.

I remember years ago a pastor friend of mine telling me something quite profound, yet without knowing the original source of these words, I have no means to quote them accurately. Further, over the years I've shared this when I've spoken and I have no doubt embellished it to take on new personal meaning. As part of the introduction of my story, I believe the following holds great truth, and hope you'll discover its relevance as you read on: "A lesson prepared in a mind will reach the minds of those taught, while a lesson prepared in the heart will reach the hearts of those who will listen, but a lesson prepared in a life will most often reach lives ..." My hope, as you read the subsequent chapters, is that your life becomes enriched and you feel encouraged as I share several of the life-impacting lessons I've learned over the years.

And so, the journey begins ...

Beginnings

I can't imagine what my parents must have thought during the first years of my life. You see, I was more than just a child with hyperactivity; I had some challenges that, quite frankly, left both my parents and the doctors quite perplexed.

From the time I could sit up on my own, I would rock back and forth. Now, that's okay if you're in a rocker, but problem was, that didn't matter to me. If I were in a chair, on the sofa, or in the back seat of the car, I would rock for hours. Even in my sleep, my father would come in and try to get me to stop bouncing my head off my pillow as I continued my rocking throughout all hours of the night. Needless to say, this caused my parents great concern, and so my mother took me to see several doctors. At first, they questioned if I was suffering from a form of autism. However, after conducting several tests, they concluded I didn't have autism, and yet they weren't able to pinpoint anything specific as the source of my constant rocking. It wasn't until one doctor in particular asked enough questions of my mother that he was able to develop a diagnosis. In short, his answer as to what I was doing was rocking to my own internal rhythm. What he told my mom would change the course of my life. His recommended prescription: "Get that boy into music."

My mother's father was a great musician in his day, and so she knew that such a suggestion wasn't too far-fetched. In fact, she took his suggestion to heart, and at age four, I began taking piano lessons at a studio which specialized in teaching young children. The name of the studio, Lo Kno Play, stood for "love, knowledge, and playing." That was the way they taught music. They instilled a love for music and imparted the knowledge to learn how to play. It wasn't just a pastime for me; it was a deep desire to learn to play music and be able to perform at their recitals as soon as I was ready. By the time I was five years old, I had played my first recital. I never recall having a fear of performing in front of people. I was more concerned about disappointing my music teacher than disappointing an audience.

I was a student there for several years. My daily routine was to wake up at 6:30 in the morning, make my bed, get dressed in my Catholic school uniform, eat breakfast, and be sitting at the piano by 7:00 a.m. so I could practice for thirty minutes before leaving for school. Monday through Friday, this was my routine, and on Saturdays my practice and chores had to be done before I could go out to play with the neighbor kids. Six days a week without fail. The only days I didn't have to practice were if I was sick, Sundays, or if we were on vacation. My sick days didn't happen very often, as my mother was a navy nurse and, let me tell you, there was no getting by her. If I didn't have a fever, I was well enough to practice.

Now don't get me wrong on this. I truly loved to practice. I just hated to make mistakes because my mom would let me know in a heartbeat. "Timmy, that's not right. Look at the music and try it again." Some days I would be in tears over the frustration of trial and error, but in the long run it sure paid off for me.

It was also during these early years that my parents often took me to local parades. I couldn't have cared less about any of the characters or floats, or costumes people were wearing. What fascinated me was the pounding of the drummers who marched by in rank and file. I wanted to be in a marching band from my first parade. I was nearly five years old, but the fact that I was already playing the piano made me hope that maybe someday I could learn to play the drums.

That desire never left me. Not for a day, not for a minute. That pounding passion became overwhelming, and I remember begging my dad over and over again to let me take drum lessons. My mother insisted I stick with piano and so, year after year, the piano vs. drum war continued. Between the ages of four and nine, I persistently begged and pleaded with my parents to let me take drum lessons. Then one day, my mom told me if I stayed with piano until I was ten years old, they would let me take drum lessons, too. I took my very first drum lesson on my tenth birthday. I didn't even have a drum yet, but the teacher brought a practice pad for me to use. These pads have a similar feel to a drum without the loud volume, which, of course, was good news to my parents.

And so the new journey of studying two musical instruments at the same time began. My daily routine had changed as well. My mother still demanded that I practiced piano every morning prior to leaving for school. But now, since my level of reading and playing had increased over the years, my practice time did as well. I had to put in forty-five minutes every morning on the piano. After school, I would come home, eat a quick snack, complete all my homework, and then do forty-five minutes of drum practice before I could even think of going out to play.

We had two pianos in our home. My brother Dennis played as well. Since he was three and a half years older than me, his skills developed much faster than mine. By the time I was eleven, he was already teaching piano to other kids in the neighborhood. I didn't like the competition of having a mother and brother who were both piano teachers, so I followed my passion and made the decision to focus on drums. After all, they were what I loved to play, and they were my strongest musical talent.

Yeah, I can remember those days so very clearly. I don't know if I will ever get over the irony of becoming totally deaf and the ramifications of that in my life as a musician. For someone who started out in music at four years of age, from my earliest recollection—my *beginnings*—I can honestly proclaim that music was my life.

The Rhythm of the Night

In my early years of drumming, I listened to lots of bands while focusing on what the drummer was playing. I became a student by hearing and studying such bands as Cream, Iron Butterfly, The Jimmy Hendrix Experience, Led Zeppelin, Blind Faith, and Emerson, Lake & Palmer. As I progressed and grew older, new artists inspired me, including Chicago, Blood Sweat & Tears, Van Halen, 38 Special, Journey, and Toto, to name a few. Over the years, I became increasingly drawn to the hardcore funk rhythms expressed by the likes of Tower of Power, Earth Wind & Fire, Cameo, and The Gap Band. I also began to target specific drummers "to go to school on," and I would play the tapes and records over and over again, until I could play their drum beats perfectly. Great drummers like Alphonse Mouzon, Billy Cobham, Zorro, Jonathan Moffett, and Ricky Lawson were some of my greatest drum teachers over the decades, and yet, I never took an actual lesson from them in person.

The reason I write of these bands and artists is because of the amount of time I listened to and played along with their drum patterns. To give you a perspective on this, from the time I began taking drum lessons at age ten up through my last days of my professional drumming, I would invest one to two hours every day, six days a week just to study and practice the various drumming rhythms. This went on for well over a twenty year period.

Listening was a huge part of my life as it related to learning my musical craft as a drummer, songwriter, and producer. For the most part, I was alone in one of my practice rooms or recording studios. Isolated from distractions with nothing but the pounding rhythms driving my focus to match the drummer, beat for beat, lick for lick. Their every drum fill, cymbal crash, downbeat and backbeat became engrained in the fiber of my soul. Even as I write this, I can go back to countless songs in my mind and tap out the rhythms as if I were practicing them just a few days ago.

Although many people have written books on the aspects of being an effective listener, I was blessed at an early age to be able to concentrate solely upon a single instrument being played in the midst of an entire band's performance. My ability to intensely focus in this manner allowed me to move beyond hearing music as a whole, and enabled me to study and learn the specific parts being played on an instrument. This entire process took years to fully develop and took incredible discipline to practice listening this way; to be able to "lock in" on the part and study away on the groove.

To say I spent thousands upon thousands of hours listening and practicing multiple styles of drumming would be an understatement. I was constantly striving to be the best performing drummer I could be, and the driving force of whatever band or group I was performing with at the time. When my day was over and I went to bed, my thoughts were endlessly focused on becoming the best; even while falling asleep I would listen to music—*the rhythm of the night.*

My Old School

Some of the great memories I have of playing music happened during my high school years. After all, I was a seventeen-year-old junior and yet, there I was, playing in nightclubs several nights a week. While most kids my age could only dream of going to a nightclub (having to wait until the age of twenty-one as the law required in California), I was already in there and loving it. Although I was permitted to perform in nightclubs, I couldn't drink any alcohol, as those establishments would have lost their liquor licenses had they served a minor. But that really wasn't a big deal for me anyhow. I "was in," and all my friends in high school thought that was so cool.

I was a very energetic player in my early years, highly animated in my playing style. I was known for following the rest of the band's "dance moves" while sitting behind my drum set. I would rock back and forth, side to side, and do lots of flashy stuff as I played. I was a huge fan of matching intensity of substance with the flash of style. I had developed several drum solos I could hammer out at any time, and each involved various theatrics. My most popular solo involved my standing up midway through and walking around my set as I played. I would go to the front of my set, stand on top of the bass drum, and reach over and continue playing with my back facing the crowd. Being a "show-off" was part of my routine and, for the most part, I was good at it because I worked hard to perfect it. Combine that with being young and cocky and often it ended in nothing but trouble!

I remember one night we were playing for a sold-out crowd and my drums were on a riser with a smaller setup than normal. Do you think that caused me to play with a little more caution? Nope, not me! I thought I was invincible on stage. So, there I was in the middle of a kickin' song, rocking back and forth on my drum throne and, next thing I knew, I fell right off the seat and all the way over the edge. From the front of the stage, I had vanished! I missed a couple of measures of the song, got back up, and started playing again. Nothing like having your ego smacked down to keep you in check. But hey, as they say, "The show must go on."

Another time we were playing at a show-club in Washington, and the stage manager got the brilliant idea to rig up a combination of fog machines, lights, and carbon dioxide fire extinguishers at the sides of and behind my drums. A thunderous explosion of white smoke, fog, and lights kicked off my drum solo. Oh yeah, this was it! A new high-level gimmick for me, and I was all about the stage presence and the wow of now. I sure wish we had practiced that whole setup a few times before we implemented it live during our performance. Not to mention, I wish that I had stayed awake during Chemistry 101. I mean, anyone with a basic understanding of chemical-based applications would think twice about what we were doing. You see, the CO2 is so cold that, most of the time, dry ice shoots out of the extinguisher in freezing foam to cool the fire. Now imagine, it was about one hundred degrees onstage from all the high wattage lights. Wham! An all-consuming explosion of four twenty pound C02 extinguishers, coupled with dry ice fog machines, engulfed me up to my neck while completely covering my drums. The end result of this embellishment was awesome to everyone in attendance. Yet to me, well, let's just say it was a numbing experience. Freezing high-pressure air blasting directly upon someone who has been barraged by 100-plus degree heat for over an hour straight is nothing to take lightly. Not to mention that one of the blasts iced me over to the point I thought I was going to lose a foot or hand. I mean to tell ya, it was one of the stupidest stunts I ever tried.

However, I wasn't about to let one little bone-chilling mishap wreck a perfectly good theatrical effect. No sir, not me. So, night after night, we kept on dazzling our crowds as best we could. Yet it was all trial and error, one miscalculation after another, and I was mostly on the receiving end. But hey! It looked cool and I was from the school of hard knocks. I was willing to take the risk for the rewards of the moment.

I had so many adventures like this. Some funny, many pretty scary, and all, without exception, were ego-driven. But the all-time most humiliating experience I had was when one of the bands I was working with during those high school days was actually asked to play the after-prom dance for *my* high school. We had already played several gigs that week, and I was beyond exhausted. We'd just finished playing a club gig that night at midnight, and the after-prom started at 2:00 a.m. We had a whole group of roadies helping out and so we were able to start on time. About an hour into the first set, we were playing a slow ballad and I was leaning over while playing to adjust one of my cymbal stands. I was so tired! I actually fell asleep while I was leaning over and slid completely out of my drum seat. I mean I went straight down to the floor and was delirious for about five minutes. Luckily for me, everyone in the band was just as tired, so there were no recriminations from any of them!

Yeah, I was embarrassed for sure, and we joked about that night for a long time. Yet how I wish I could play music again. How I would welcome being so physically exhausted from playing a thumping set of tunes that I'd fall to sleep while playing and fall off the stage ... but I realize I can't go back. There is no way to turn back the hands of time. No use in pretending I'll ever return to *my old school.*

Who Let the Dogs Out?

There was at a time when it was next to impossible to go to a football game without hearing the song "Who Let the Dogs Out" by the pop group The Baja Men. Theme songs have rocked stadiums and various sporting venues for decades. Songs like "Let's Get It Started" by The Black Eyed Peas, "We Are the Champions" by Queen, and, of course, "Celebration" by Kool & The Gang are just a few examples of theme songs embraced by both fans and athletes.

Some teams have even gone on to record their own songs. The Chicago Bears recorded "The Super Bowl Shuffle" and made a video to accompany the hit single. The San Francisco 49ers also recorded a 45 RPM hit single. No doubt, there are other players who launched brief successes as musical acts, capitalizing on their athletic accomplishments and celebrity.

But the team that stands out for me for such an attempt is the San Diego Chargers group "hi-five." Many people don't realize that five players from the San Diego Chargers came together as a vocal group to record an entire album. The songs were flavored with

R&B and pop, and the lyrics were plays on words of football lingo for the most part. The album's title is *The Other Side of Us*, and the cover is of the five players in black tuxedos with the stadium in the background. It is a night shot, and above the stadium a piercing lightning bolt illuminates the picture.

You may wonder how I know so much about this particular project. Well, I was fortunate enough to be called by the album's producer and asked to record a couple of drum tracks for the project. It was totally different from anything I had ever done before. This was a group of five guys who were arguably some of the best professional football players of their day, and I was a part of their musical endeavor.

Reflecting back on working on that project brings back so many fond memories. It happened at a time when I was recording a great deal and working on several musical projects at once. It was truly an honor to be asked to be a part of this record, and it will always hold a special memory for me.

It's funny how we can get wrapped up in so many things and, at the time, not give much thought to all we are involved in. This is how it was for me. I was gigging all the time in those days, and this was just another gig, another recording. Yet now, I look back and I'm so grateful for all those days of work.

Don't get me wrong here. Some of the groups and artists I worked with were at best a real challenge. Attitudes and pretentious posers galore, but thank goodness, they were far and few between for me. Most of the folks I worked with had amazing talent and left the "prima donna" persona someplace else.

Times have certainly changed for me when it comes to going to a sporting event or concert. I now only observe the thunderous ovations and celebrations of the home team scoring through others' reactions, not through sound. Standing ovations at sold-out concerts are nothing more than a leg stretch for me, as I don't feel the excitement or thrill from the roar of the crowd. There is an eerie calm in such venues, and the absence of voices leaves me with an odd feeling of something missing. It's not just the loud noise of the crowd I miss. It's the effect of thousands upon thousands of crazed fans screaming at the top of their lungs, which promotes a euphoric feeling, not just for the players, but for those in attendance. A thunderous crowd can become contagious. Think of the wave. It starts with just a few fans and, before long, an entire stadium of sixty, seventy thousand people all participate in rising and sitting, which comprises the motion of the wave.

Sporting events and concerts are filled with a vast number of sounds. From tailgate music as diverse as the food being cooked up in the parking lot to the cheers, the chants, and the praises given to the performers. Whether athlete or musician, when someone takes the stage, the crowd goes wild. Beyond that explosion of sound, it's also the accompaniment of noises made by the motley collection of an enthusiastic crowd that often makes people want to go to games and concerts. After all, you can watch any number of ball games on the television. You can buy or download concert footage of your favorite bands any time. Let's be real; the most exciting part of such events is being a part of the multitude. Being there live, up front and personal—that makes all the difference. It's being there in the midst of that exhilarating, heart-pounding frenzy that makes you jump to your feet and shout, "*Who let the dogs out?*"

Urgent

Have you ever had a voicemail message where the calling party needed you to return their call ASAP? Not just for the sake of making it seem important, but because it really was a matter of paramount concern?

Although it's been nearly fifteen years since I received such a voicemail, I remember it as though it was last week. I had just finished a business meeting in Los Angeles and was driving home on the freeway, heading south to San Diego on a Friday afternoon. I use the term "driving" loosely, as the traffic was horrible, which is typical during rush hours along Interstate 5. Nonetheless, even at a mere ten to fifteen miles per hour, I was making headway toward home.

It had been a long week with more than the usual number of meetings, two of them out of town. So, by this point in the week I was tired, both physically and mentally. Not to mention, I had just had an MRI the week prior and was waiting on the results. I knew something was going on inside of me that wasn't quite right, and anticipating the test results was wearing on me.

Somewhere in the midst of listening to a CD and checking my voicemails in the stop-and-go drive, I got *the call*. It was from the doctor who ordered several of my tests, including the MRI. I can still play the tape of that call in my mind. "Hi Tim, this is Doctor Stearns. Will you please call me as soon as possible so we can discuss your MRI results?"

Now, if you've ever had an MRI and nothing shows up, doctors usually leave that good news on your voicemail. After all, there's no need to call back since they can just tell you, "Everything looks fine." But when they find something irregular or concerning, there's a different aspect to the conversation. The doctors aren't going to leave that kind of information on a voicemail or with anyone but the patient.

I was nervous about returning his call and so I put it off until I returned to my office late that afternoon. I remember walking in the door with tunnel vision to avoid my staff and making it straight to my office with no conversations. I sat down and took a couple of deep breaths and then dialed. I thought for sure since it was after 4:00 p.m. on a Friday, my doctor would be gone for the weekend and I could put off the conversation until the following Monday. Well, much to my amazement, the doctor picked up the phone within a couple of rings and told me he was waiting for my call.

"Hi, Mr. Mauricio, this is Doctor Stearns and we have the results back from your MRI scan." I remember his voice being very somber and, as I was about to find out, his tone was most appropriate. "We've found a large tumor on the right side of your brain. In addition to its obstruction of the auditory nerve, it's also very close to the brainstem. I have reviewed this with our medical experts who specialize in brain tumors, and we've determined you'll need to have brain surgery immediately to remove the tumor."

Over the course of our fifteen minute conversation, he explained that this would be about an eight to nine hour surgery and I would be in the hospital for five to six days, depending on my rate of recovery. They would try their best to preserve my hearing on the right side but couldn't guarantee me success due to the size and proximity of the tumor. He provided me with the names and phone numbers of the other doctors who would handle my surgery and encouraged me to follow up first thing Monday morning to schedule an appointment and a surgery date.

Monday morning arrived, and my wife and I met with one of the specialists who would be part of the surgical team. We learned that he was one of the foremost specialists in the country working with patients who suffer from these types of brain tumors. During our consultation, he explained to us that I had an extremely rare neurological disease called Neurofibromatosis type 2, commonly referred to as NF2. Upon reviewing the MRI scan, my doctor pointed out a secondary brain tumor on my left auditory nerve, as well as one in my neck. However, for now, the team wanted to solely focus on the surgery at hand and would address the other tumors at a future date.

The paramount concern for them was removing the tumor before it reached the brainstem. Not opting for surgery would pose a significant risk of the tumor growing into the brainstem. If it did so, it would affect all life functions and prove fatal.

Looking back, it's funny how two words can have so much impact on your life. Two words can suddenly create an entire shift in your strategic thinking and planning. Two words can change the focus of your daily activities, the words you choose in speaking to your loved ones, the friends you want to see, the things in life you wish you could take back. Those two words for me were "brain tumors." It was so hard for me to conceptualize that this was actually happening to me. My life was being impacted by something far beyond my control. It wasn't due to anything I was responsible for, or in any way something I could change on my own.

I still go through yearly MRI scans to see if any new tumors are developing or if there are any other signs of NF2-related issues. These are coupled with appointments with my neurologist every two months. I still feel a bit of anxiety each time I go for an MRI or CT scan, praying and trusting in God that I won't receive an e-mail or text communication with the word "urgent."

Monophobia

Yeah, this is actually both a song and an actual word to describe a fear someone might have. For me, the word "monophobia" likewise plays a dual role in illustrating two of my experiences.

To clarify, one of the definitions of this word is "Having acute fear of being alone and having to cope without a specific person, or perhaps any person, in close proximity."[1] This is highly true of persons who suffer from ongoing anxiety and panic attacks. These are something I frequently deal with and, without exception, I hate being alone when they occur. After all, it's not as if I can just dial the phone and talk to a live body and hear a human voice on the other end.

Yet a more personalized definition of this word describes what I was facing on a daily basis. A *phobia* typically means "an extreme fear of something." Now, the word *mono* in the music world describes the transmission of sound through one channel and is

---

1 http://anxietycare.org.uk/docs/fear_of_being_alone Monophobia - accessed April 7th, 2012

the opposite of *stereo*. In other words, you are only hearing from one side. To go from an AM radio system of transmission to stereo sound is amazing. The depth and richness of the music is truly wonderful. However, the opposite holds true when going from the amazing complexities and depth of stereo to only mono.

Just imagine the difference between experiencing the depth of the sound achieved through such high-end systems at many movie theaters, and then going to a handheld radio with a little speaker. Shocking to say the least, right? Well, that's precisely what was going on for me in my thinking. The fear of not hearing in both ears was a source of incredible trepidation. It was my fear, my deepest fear, the monophobia of only being able to hear musical sounds and conversations from one side.

You see, for the vast majority of people, hearing in stereo is just the norm. It's nothing uncommon, nothing extraordinary, nothing to write home about, because after all, doesn't pretty much everybody hear in stereo?

Yep, that's just the way I viewed things for nearly thirty-nine years. I never thought about going through life and not hearing in stereo. Losing my hearing in one ear wasn't even on my radar. I never really paid attention to those persons who had any sort of hearing disorders because I naively thought, "If they can't hear the music I'm playing, then we don't have much in common, anyhow." Oh man! It can be absolutely shocking how quickly the sudden changes in life can bring about a reality check.

After my first brain surgery, the setbacks were tough, to say the least. Within several hours of the surgery, while still in the ICU, one of the first things my wife told me, besides the fact that I made it through the surgery and was going to be okay, was that the tumor on the right side of my brain was wrapped around the auditory nerve and the doctors couldn't save my hearing on that side.

During those first days in the hospital and while recovering at home, all sorts of other things began to become a reality for me. I developed permanent facial paralysis on the right side and severe ringing in my ear from the nerve being destroyed. But it took weeks for me to settle into being deaf in one ear. It was surreal, and for the most part I was in denial. In my innermost thoughts, I was holding on to the hope that the nerve would miraculously grow back and my hearing would be restored. As the days turned into weeks and weeks into months, my hopes faded as I came to grips with the reality of being permanently deaf in that ear. The auditory nerve that once provided me with a sense of hearing was suddenly replaced with incredibly loud ringing. Like feedback at a concert, it was a brutal fact, one I needed to accept and learn to live with.

Let me attempt to share with you what this is like in a way you can most likely relate.

I would assume you've been to a couple, if not several concerts (or musical performances) in your lifetime. Under this assumption, I'd guess it would be fair to say you've undoubtedly experienced "feedback." Be it from a microphone or instrument, it's that high-pitched screeching sound that makes you cover your ears. It's loud and painful, and you instinctively go to cover (and protect) your hearing with a rapid reflex. Well, that's what I was hearing and continue to hear daily, as a result of that first surgery.

One of the most frequent questions I'm asked these days is, "If you're deaf, how can you hear ringing?" It's weird to think about and even more frustrating to live with. Believe me! The "feedback" and ringing sensations are unbearable at times. Only strong sedatives, which make me sleep, help take the noise away. Most mornings, it's what causes me to wake up long before the sun rises.

Let me tell you, no matter how frustrated I was back in the days of hearing in only one ear, I was ignorant for not appreciating what

I had at that time. What was once a great fear for me, "*monophobia,*" as I use the word, I would today receive as a welcomed blessing!

Yakety Yak

In 1958, Jerry Leiber and Mike Stoller wrote, produced, and arranged a song for The Coasters, which has become a timeless classic. It was the same year I was born, and for me to say that I grew up with this song is a matter of fact.

The lyrics depict the culture of the youth then and they still hold today. From those who tried to follow James Dean, Marlon Brando, and every other actor who portrayed the essence of wild and free, the predominate attitude was one of rebellion. That was no more present than in the way they communicated.

"Don't talk back!" You can hardly help using these words as a parent when your kids start yappin' at you with excuses about this and that, one thing or another, communicating their disregard for what you asked them to do. From taking out the trash to cleaning up their rooms, parents set forth certain expectations, household rules, and expect them to be done without being talked back to by their children.

The five words in this song, which have now become famous, have also become descriptive of something which occurs almost every day in my life. "Yakety yak" is what I continually observe while watching other people talk with one another. Lips moving at the speed of light with hands and arms flapping. It's really a different world living in continual silence and watching others' conversations.

In another context, it's the "don't talk back" that has become a significant challenge for me to overcome. I can be at a store, or sitting in a restaurant or coffee shop, and as I take the time to look about, I often will see someone close by who looks agitated with me. As if I just offended them with something I said. All too often, people will say something to me and then when I "don't talk back," they think I'm being rude or putting them off. To complicate matters, I actually do fairly well at speechreading, or "lipreading", with many people. At times, I'm able to follow certain people who are looking right at me when they're talking, while other times I may not respond to those who are talking at me and unaware of my being totally deaf ... can you appreciate the situation?

I've actually had people want to get into a physical confrontation over my not responding to them. I can only imagine some of the words they threw out at me before getting close up in my face where I could follow what they were saying. I remember one of those incidents as if it were yesterday. It was just two days before my second brain surgery, and I had just stepped out of my car at the mall. As I turned around, a guy with long hair and a nasty-looking beard was sitting on his bike and talking to me. I couldn't follow a single word he was saying and so I explained to him I was deaf. He got really irritated and as clear as a bell said, "bull—." He turned and as he rode away was still yelling out stuff and then extended his right arm and hand with middle finger in the air. Well, he just caught me at a point where I was really frustrated in life and had about hit my limit. Actually, I think he pushed me over that limit, and so, without restraint, I yelled at him, "Hey you punk. You don't know me and don't you ever flip me off." With that, he turned around on his bike and came back a few spaces. Then, trying to intimidate me, he threw his bike down, walked a few steps toward me, and with his arms flaying and mouth moving, he uttered words I could only imagine. In my momentary rage and loss of control, I yelled at this guy and told him I would bust him up if he didn't get out of my face. Well, thank God he did, and although I can look back on this and tell it as more of a funny story, it truly was one of the oddest things to occur as a result of my being deaf.

Yet in all fairness to that creep on the bike and to those persons who become upset and challenge my deafness, I realize their responses stem from my ability to speak as a normally hearing person speaks. After all, I was a hearing person for most of my life and my verbal communication has never diminished .

It's amazing how we all just live life with the assumption that every other person in this world has all of their senses and faculties. That is, unless there are outward physical indicators, which allow us to conclude otherwise.

On the flip side, having raised two children who are now adults, my wife and I have sure had our experiences dealing with the phrase "Don't talk back to me." I can remember times when my son or daughter would push me past my limit, and in exasperation I would yell, "Would you just shut up?" Oh man, am I ever regretful for those words! I wish I could take them back and though I've asked each of my children for their forgiveness,(both when those times happened and since), I wish I'd never, ever said "shut up." Even the words "don't talk back" are now contrary to what I feel a lot of the time. Not in the sense of their arguing or rebelling against what we would advise (keep in mind our children are now adults), but more from just being able to hear them express their opinions about life.

It's interesting to me how often most of us at one time or another have either wanted to or actually told someone to "shut up." Other times, we may have found ourselves getting to the point of yelling out, "Leave me alone!" But then, when life dramatically changes and you find yourself unable to use the sense that allowed you to hear all that noise, talking, racket and *yakety yak* in the first place ... well, I'm just sayin'.

Rockin' Down the Highway

There's nothing quite like driving down the road with great weather and tunes blasting. I could drive for hours on end on cross-country trips for business and burn up ten to twelve CDs in a day just listening to all kinds of music. From hard rock to old-school funk, jazz to ballads and lots of Christian artists, I would easily click off eight hundred plus miles in a single day.

In my encounters with people from all walks of life, I've yet to meet someone who doesn't like music on some level. That is, except for those who were born deaf. In most regards, for the deaf, music is a foreign concept. Although lyrics can be appreciated, they really are no more than poetry or a story to a non-hearing person. The concept of melodies coupled with layers of vast sounds driven by complex rhythms is something which can only be totally appreciated by one who has hearing. Trust me on this, as I know what I'm talking about. It's one of those true life situations that applies to the saying, "You can't miss what you never had."

It's both interesting and emotionally difficult to sit in a vehicle and watch the person who is driving me around, realizing they are jammin' to the sounds of some great music. I can see their head and lips moving and know they are enjoying the sounds that fill the air. It's something that requires me to be only a spectator of their movements and vibrations, while forcing myself to respect the groove they're enjoying.

Sometimes, I'll ask what CD they've got in the player. If it's one of those I used to listen to frequently back when I had hearing, I will try to guess the song based upon the rhythm I feel from the door or subwoofer. When I can guess those songs correctly, I immediately turn my attention to the power of memory and give thanks to God for providing me with such an amazing ability to recall hundreds of songs from my past. It's the one part of my memory that is still crystal clear and sharp, unlike many other areas of my recollection that are foggy at best.

It's amazing how many people like driving me around these days. I guess that's because they can blast the tunes without me ever saying, "Turn that down," plus the fact that they know I'll never complain about their singing or the music they're playing.

Yep, I have to tell ya, there's just nothing like having all the windows down, the wind blowing on your face at seventy miles per hour, and tunes blasting at the threshold of the vehicle's sound system. I used to drive like that in the summer all the time. The air conditioner on full blast and hot air blowin' around ... friends used to call me "cool breeze" because of that style I adopted when driving. Heck, I'd do the opposite at nighttime with the heater on and the cold air blowing in from outside. Regardless of the temperature outside, the windows in my rides were always down and the tunes were blazing loud. Man, those were good days!

So, now even though the experience of cruising down the road is entirely different for me, at least I can embrace the moments of watching my family and friends enjoy cranking tunes in the car. My son, who is an amazing drummer, reminds me of myself in those days gone by. I love riding with him, as he always has the windows down and music thumping. I just have to say it: "There's truly nothing quite like being in a car and *rockin' down the highway.*"

Message in a Bottle

Back in the days when I had my hearing, it was common for friends of mine, who were fighting colds or severe allergies, to complain about how difficult it was for them to hear. I was no different. When people are faced with a sudden challenge to hear at their normal capacity, it becomes difficult at best for them to remain passive. Frustrations galore can set in for each person as they try to remedy their individual predicaments.

Come on now, you know how it is when you wake up with a stuffed-up nose and your ears feel like you just got out of a swimming pool. Fluid is swashing around, so you start to shake your head from side to side, as if something is actually going to come out! The next attempt may be to take something like a decongestant or antihistamine to try to dry up the condition. Yep, I've been there and done that, let me tell you. But for me it wasn't just a couple of days I felt like this. No, my condition was for the better part of two years. It was relentless, day in and day out.

I guess the best way to sum up this time period would be to say, "I was desperately seeking a remedy." For me, "desperation" is a word, which describes "the most paramount of desire arising from one's despair." At least, that's what was going on for me during 2004 and the better part of 2005. I mean, I was already deaf in one ear and struggling with severe ringing on my right side from the auditory nerve damage in my brain. Over the seven years which had passed since my previous surgery, I was dealing with the slow effects of the hearing in my left ear being destroyed by the tumor on that side. Oh, let me tell you, there are probably only a few folks who have become as desperate as I did in my attempts to overcome my frustrations and concerns.

Every single day, I would wake up and begin to talk to myself in the bathroom to get a "sound check." I would say words like "hello" and "what" over and over again, checking to see if I could hear my own voice. As days progressed to weeks, I experimented with various home remedies to try to fix my problem. Because, after all, that's what we guys think we can do in life, "fix the problem." So, I started with acupressure to see if I could get some relief. When that didn't work out for me, I moved to having acupuncture and tried various herbal teas and concoctions.

But my desperate endeavors didn't end there. I went to my doctor and tried several rounds of steroid taper treatments. Oh man, I've got to say that the stuff I was taking was brutal! I gained weight and puffed up about thirty pounds, not to mention that my temper flared at the littlest and stupidest things. The side effects from the steroids became so frustrating for me that I also started taking diuretics to clear up any possible fluid in my inner ear.

After several months of trying all these various plans to eradicate my hearing challenges to no avail, I even asked my doctor if he would put a tube in my ear to help with the pressure and any potential fluid. He agreed it couldn't hurt anything, but was not real hopeful. The underlying cause of all these things I was experiencing was the large brain tumor now growing on the left side of my brain which was destroying my hearing. As my doctor told me more than once, "Tim, I feel for you and I know this is a slow torture for you."

Nothing, and I mean nothing, was working. I purchased two different state of the art digital hearing aids, the best on the market at that time. Although they did provide me with some help, it was a daily struggle for me. Every day, and I mean each and every single morning, I would put the hearing aid in my ear, walk out of my bedroom, so as to not wake up my wife, and then start to do a sound check. After a few weeks, I got to the point where I was able to perform my morning sound checks and determine if I was going to have a good or bad day hearing.

There I was, a senior executive in the company I worked for, faced with the prospect of knowing each day if it was going to be a "good day" or a "tough day" for meetings and phone calls. I did everything I could to overcome the challenges. As often as possible I used e-mail instead of phone calls and made sure everyone around me knew to look at me and speak slower than normal so I could do my best to lipread. The best way to describe the sounds and words I was hearing is to say it was as though they were coming through a glass bottle. Distorted and echoing, as if I was trying to listen to a crappy fast food speaker box when ordering food. Whatever I was hearing, at best it was like a message in a bottle.

For almost two solid years, this went on each and every day for me. All the while, in the back of my mind, I was faced with the stark reality that the tumor was growing and would eventually overtake my ability to hear.

Desperate to hear? You bet!

Afraid of becoming totally deaf? No question about it!

The value on wanting to have my hearing back? Priceless!

That was the *"message in a bottle"* to me!

Weird Science

I grew up watching science fiction programs on television and going to countless sci-fi movies. I mean, I look back on those now and laugh at most of the make-believe technology, but some of what I used to watch and thought totally impossible to come to fruition is now low-tech by comparison.

In 1985, the movie *Weird Science,* written and directed by John Hughes, portrayed two high school geeks who developed a science project which allowed them to create the ultimate woman of their dreams. The movie's theme song, "Weird Science" by Oingo Boingo, was a big hit and got a lot of radio airtime.

In searching for a chapter title to describe the technological aspects of my journey, the song "Weird Science" really sums them up.

Perhaps you may recall the long-running television series *Star Trek: The Next Generation* with actor LeVar Burton. His character, Geordi La Forge, was blind, but by wearing a special visor, could see with greater clarity than those with normal vision. Far-fetched and over-the-top to believe in real life, but hey, that's what sci-fi is all about, right? To make the unbelievable seem believable and bring it to life. It's all about the weird science.

What if there were the technology and medical capabilities to make a deaf person hear? What if that wasn't sci-fi, but in fact a reality? Surely, it would be worthwhile to investigate. After all, I was at a point in my life where I would be willing to do most anything to get my hearing back. I was desperate to hear again after a few short months of being totally deaf. I couldn't imagine at that point in time trying to live the remainder of my life without sound, without voices, without music.

Developed by Cochlear, there is a device called "PABI," which stands for Penetrating Auditory Brainstem Implant. The technology at that time was new to the public, yet well into advanced stages of its development. If I decided to go through the experimental surgery, I would be the seventh person to ever receive this device. It is hard-wired into the brainstem with penetrating electrodes and connected to a receiver, which is placed behind the ear under the scalp. Through extremely high-end technology, the receiver picks up sounds and sends them to the brainstem to help with various sound recognition applications.

When the device is working properly, the brain receives sounds, which can best be described as series of "beeps and boops." Reportedly, over time, the brain is able to retrain itself, and these sounds often assist the individual in certain daily activities. For some, it is proven to be of great value. For others, it's been reported to bring moderate compensation compared to total deafness.

Having been tested by several doctors at the time and having my case being reviewed my various medical experts around the country, my name was submitted as a potential candidate for the surgery. After months of waiting to be on the recipient list for the device and to find out if I'd be approved for the surgery, my wife received a call from the doctors to learn I was finally approved. We went ahead with the surgery with high hopes for a positive outcome.

With the greatest of intentions on everyone's part, the ensuing months would reveal that I was not so fortunate. In point of fact, it was quite the opposite. Ultimately, the PABI created a whole set of disabling challenges for me that are now permanent. The major connective wire from the receiver to the brainstem moved and ended up on my facial nerve, which has caused me to suffer from ongoing hemifacial spasms. Although medications and Botox injections every two months help me to deal with this, it is a significant challenge to say the least. I was never able to receive consistent transmissions from the receiver that was designed to aid my ability to perceive speech or sound. Since the wire moved and became attached to the nerve, the receiver frequently sent an electronic shock through my head, resulting in excruciating shooting pains throughout the left side of my face and eyes during initial stages of use. And so, after months of testing and evaluation, the neurosurgeon who performed my surgery decided to discontinue any further testing or use of the device. After high hopes for being a part of this experimental program, the results for me were unfortunately disappointing.

Medical breakthroughs and technological advancements are often perceived as science fiction brought to reality. But even with such amazing accomplishments, the reality can be less than what the individual hoped to receive. Sometimes the results are nothing short of miraculous, and other times they can be devastating. What happened to me was the latter. Both the physical torment and emotional discouragement will be a lifelong battle. Yet the wonders of medical science as a result of those who dedicate their lives to such advancements should be embraced. They should be applauded for their commitment to achieve the unthinkable and to bringing into reality that which we often view as nothing more than "*weird science.*"

Double Vision

When I first came out of recovery from my second brain surgery and could see my wife for the first time, my eyes felt like they were on a roller coaster. They where going from side to side, up and down, and all I could make out was two of everything. This visual sensation is a condition called oscillopsia. It was the worst thing I could have imagined to happen. There I was, deaf as deaf can be, and on top of that, I had no visual capacity. I could only make out my wife's face for a few seconds and then had to close my eyes for minutes at a time to try to focus again. It was without a doubt the most helpless feeling I had ever had. To be in ICU, trying to communicate when I couldn't hear or focus my eyes to see anyone was no fun at all!

As the evening progressed, the sensation subsided just enough that I could focus for about fifteen to thirty seconds at a time without my eyes bouncing around in my head, but I still had really bad double vision. I've always tried to keep a good sense of humor about all this stuff, and so when the doctor came in to talk to my wife, he wrote down his questions for me in huge letters, asking me what I saw when trying to look around the room. I replied, "Two of everything, and that now, my wife looks twice as beautiful." He laughed and thought that was a great line. It was, and it was true.

When you go through any type of brain surgery, there's always a bunch of potential risks. I never thought much about the visual risks because of being so focused on hearing-related outcomes. But when those potential risks become reality, it's amazing how quickly a precautionary list of side effects is suddenly a huge deal. I can't begin to describe how frustrating it is, not to mention how challenging and utterly frightening it is to be totally deaf and have significant visual impairments with which to contend. The two of these combined sure make most days a real challenge.

Nothing could have prepared me for what I now deal with on a daily basis. Deafness is incredible isolating. It removes a person from being a part of many activities in life. I can be in a room full of people and yet feel alone, as I have no specific connection points with conversations. Even when someone just listens to others, there is the connection being made, a feeling of being a part of what's being shared. That's what conversation is all about—someone talking and someone listening. So, as a deaf person, unless I have someone facing me and that person is talking directly to me, I'm not a part of the conversation. Helen Keller was once quoted as saying, "Blindness separates us from things, but deafness separates us from people." How true I have found this over my life.

But it's more than that. Let me illustrate something for you. Picture yourself at the beach. There you are, reclining in your beach chair. The waves are crashing along the shore, and kids are running into the water and screaming as the waves of cold water hit them. Seagulls fly overhead, and you hear their calls and their wings flapping. People on skateboards roll down the sidewalk, and the wheels make that all-too distinctive sound. While basking in the warm sunshine, surrounding and distant conversations fill the air, and as you listen to all of this, you have that quintessential feeling of spending a day at the beach and all is well.

You see, for a deaf person, there is none of that. I have to remind myself of each of those sounds. Often, I will ask my wife when we are at the beach or someplace similar, "What do you hear, honey?", "Tell me all that you're hearing right now." This helps me to remember, but it's not the same. Nothing can ever replace all those sounds.

As an experiment, try this some time: go to a public place like the beach, or a park and sit there for a bit. Then write down everything you hear. Close your eyes and focus on every sound you take in over the period of five or ten minutes. Then imagine that you'll never hear it again.

One of the positive aspects of my being deaf is my newfound joy and sincere appreciation of still being able to see with my eyes, even though I do struggle greatly with double vision and oscillopsia. I remind myself often that even the most troublesome days of experiencing visual disorders are a blessing compared to the thought of being blind along with being deaf. I am so grateful to God for allowing me to still be able to view the world around me. It's really caused me to see life in a much different way. I've gained a new ability to "listen" with my eyes, where I once listened with my ears. To see and hear with my eyes gives additional new meaning to the words "*double vision.*"

Soul Vaccination

In those former years of my constant pursuit of developing my skills as a drummer and teaching myself how to duplicate the exact drumming styles of various artists, there were few more difficult songs for me to master than those from the band Tower of Power. One of the most difficult tunes I ever had to learn was called "Soul Vaccination." The band's drummer at that time was David Garibaldi. His ability to lay down a groove with the utmost syncopation forced anyone who attempted to duplicate his rhythmic patterns to really have to "go to school" on what he was doing in order to play the parts with the same precision.

I can remember so vividly the first time I sat down behind my drums with headphones on and engaged the same sticking and footwork that David so masterfully played. Challenged to say the least, it took me weeks to learn to play that one song. I remember being so agitated when I couldn't figure out precisely what he was doing. I was perplexed and overwhelmed to say the least. There was no way for me to watch him in person as a student or read a drum chart for what he played. The song was just out on record, and the only way for me to learn it was to listen and play. It was one of those songs (and there were only a few for me) that I almost gave up trying to learn. It was almost too great an effort to invest in just one song.

In a relevant comparison, after having gone through two brain surgeries and contending with all the setbacks and physical impairments caused by the surgeries' complications and NF2 itself, I find myself frequently being overwhelmed and perplexed while trying to cope with the never-ending adjustments.

Throughout the day, I fight with the loss of being able to focus my eyes, due to double vision and suffering from severe oscillopsia. The impact from this one disability alone is enough to make a person go crazy. This came about as a result of significant damage incurred by the optic nerves, caused both by the tumors and related surgeries. If you have no knowledge of what it is like for people who are afflicted with this condition, well, let me just tell you it is nothing short of horrific. When someone with normal vision is walking, driving, or moving about, their eyes remain focused (steady) on the object or objects they are looking at. But with severe oscillopsia, the object or objects of focus bounce. For example, when riding in a car, especially at night, all of the lights bounce around as though I were watching popcorn pop in a kettle. It's so frustrating that most of the time I have to close my eyes to make the dancing lights stop.

Then there's the continual struggle of trying to live with profound dizziness. This literally causes me to routinely bump into objects, frequently to lose my balance completely, and creates the ongoing sensation of feeling nauseous.

Another significant challenge is the frequent hemifacial spasms caused by the wire, inserted during my second brain surgery, which penetrates my brainstem and goes to the implant under my scalp.

Within a few months of this surgery, the wire inexplicably moved and decided to find a home on my facial nerve. The spasms are so intense they can only be managed with Botox injections every eight weeks, along with medication to control the spasms. Without ongoing treatments, my face would look like it had a fishhook stuck in the side of my mouth and someone was going to reel me in!

Yet, even through all of this, one the most difficult things for me to adjust to is the emotional aspect of loss. I lost the sense of hearing, one I'd had my entire life, and I realized I had taken that ability, that God-given sense for granted. I mean, it was just part of who I was. I never knew any young person, or even someone under seventy-five years of age, who had become deaf. Did I know people who were hard of hearing? Yeah, for sure, but not totally deaf! The reality for me was that I never even knew a single person who was deaf. Deafness itself or for that matter, even knowing someone who was deaf on a personal level was as foreign to me as people living in Tanzania. I knew Tanzanians existed, but I never had been there and never met anyone from there. So, it was all just far off and non-applicable to me.

It's truly amazing to me how much my perspective about things has changed. Those matters which I gave little thought to before now have my utmost attention. What was once a very foreign concept of which I was remotely aware, is now front and center for me each and every day. Thinking about my inner complaints while endlessly listening to especially difficult drumming patterns or songs, or those times I resisted listening to styles of music which took me far out of my comfort zone, I now realize just how precious those days truly were for me. All I have to do is pause for a moment and reflect back on that which I took so much for granted, and I see the blessings I still have right in front of me today. Somehow in all of this, it's in those moments of contemplation that I find a different form of peace and inspiration. I like to think of them as my time of having another *soul vaccination*.

Hold on for One More Day

This sure is a fitting song title for what I was going through the few years prior to my second brain surgery. It was beyond nerve-racking to face the daily challenges of whether or not I could make out the voices of others as audibly understandable speech. As I mentioned in an earlier chapter, I never knew from hour to hour if I was going to be able to have a conversation based upon my ability to hear or not.

Within a few weeks of this dramatic change in my ability to hear conversations, I realized I had better come up with some alternative solutions in order to continue my professional responsibilities with minimal disruptions. And so, I developed various plans of attack related to each of my job functions. As a senior executive overseeing a team of talented individuals, I was entrusted with the leadership responsibility of developing our company's business—bottom line, its revenue.

The core product or service we provided was in the arena of helping financial institutions grow their lending portfolios. We accomplished this by providing credit unions with a competitive vehicle-leasing program to offer their local area automotive dealerships. The credit unions would secure and utilize our company's expertise in being both the vehicle lessor and program administrator. Besides maintaining current business relationships, we also met with prospective clients throughout the country. Thus, part of my job involved traveling around the country and meeting with both existing clients and prospects.

After flying a few cross-country trips, I soon realized that the altitude changes upon takeoff and decent had a significant negative impact on me. The cabin pressure changes caused my hearing to virtually be gone for a few days and impaired my balance. These two physical challenges were demoralizing. Besides the physical impact, there was the frustration in dealing with all this.

One day I was talking to our corporate attorney, and he informed me that he never flew and always traveled by train. What a revelation that was for me! From that time forward, I stopped flying and either took the train or drove a rented car to my meetings. Now, when I say I drove, I mean I *drove*. Over the better part of five years, I drove all over the United States. From coast to coast, both north and south, east and west.

You see, taking the train was great, but it didn't stop very frequently when traveling across the country. Not at the places I needed to stop, anyhow. Hence, I was becoming a cross-country driver for business. I would often leave home on a Friday and drive fourteen plus hours per day for three straight days in order to be at a meeting twenty-five hundred miles from my home. Then, I would drive that entire week to various meetings and conclude on a Thursday in order to drive all day Friday, Saturday, and Sunday to return home and start the next week.

But that was just part of the challenge. I had such difficulty making out conversations that I would always need to have someone from our team with me. I needed someone to type out the business conversations in real time on a laptop in order for me to follow along. On several of my two-week trips, my wife traveled with me, helping me in hotel settings and restaurants. Simple things like ordering food, checking into a hotel, or asking directions were all a crapshoot for me, and so I was dependent upon having help in order to ensure success.

One time, while we were in San Antonio, Texas, I had an unusual and humorous experience. On this particular trip, I had several scheduled meetings throughout both the Southern and Eastern states. My itinerary on this trek called for me to travel for three weeks, and so I decided to take my family with me in our motor home. It was summer and the kids were out of school. I thought it would be good for us as a family and also a productive time for me. So, there we were, the second night on our trip in our hotel, and it was in the middle of the night. I woke up and needed a drink of water. I thought I'd be polite and not turn on any lights so as to not disturb the family. I walked into the bathroom in the dark, went to close the door, and in backing up, I tripped over the bathtub, hit my head against the wall, and collapsed into the tub with my feet hanging over the edge.

Yep, there I was. Mister Courteous! In my shorts, feet hanging out and over the tub, and I was all but knocked out from slamming my head against the wall. It must have taken me five minutes or better to just get out of that stupid tub. At that moment, I realized how bad my balance issues were becoming, and in the dark, I was nothing short of a danger to myself. From that time on, the bathroom light was left on for me. I didn't want to end up in a newspaper headline, "Man collapses in tub with serious brain damage as a result of not leaving a light on."

Although we laughed about that situation for the entire trip and for years after, it was truly the beginning of my realization that my condition was becoming worse. It wasn't as though one massive thing happened and then I had to deal with the result. It was a very slow process, and each day presented its own set of challenges.

I went from having telephone conversations to using e-mail. I would be sure to have people face me directly when talking to me to enhance my ability to read their lips. Someone was always with me to either type or write out the conversation's bullet points so I could keep up. It was beyond a challenge as my physical situation was equally met with emotional pressure to endure and not fail.

Even with the most advanced hearing aids, medical interventions, and medicines, nothing proved to be successful against the destructive power of brain tumors caused by NF2. It truly was in those days, much as it is now, all I could do to *hold on for one more day.*

Hold on Loosely

One of my favorite rock and roll bands was 38 Special. If I had to choose which song I listened to the most by this group, it would be "Hold on Loosely." So, in searching for a song to fit this chapter title, well, this just came easily to me.

I'm one of those kinds of people who could be described as having a somewhat tenacious personality. Like a dog with a bone, when I grab a hold of something, I don't like to let go, and I am not much for surrendering anything I'm passionate about. I don't ever recall embracing the philosophy of "easy come, easy go."

Part of the journey I've been through has shown me a lot about myself regarding my tenacious behavior. This is coupled with my tendency to be obsessive-compulsive. Most of us who have these traits don't fare well with change unless we are convinced it's for the betterment of our lives; most certainly, we don't like be forced to give up anything we've worked incredibly hard to achieve.

The shock and awe of experiencing any significant loss is hard enough to deal with. But when you add to this compounding losses brought about by circumstances beyond your control, it can feel unbearable. That's exactly what happened to me.

I can attest to the surreal experience of being abandoned by those who were close to me in business and business-related friendships. One of my dear friends at the time completely shifted his thinking regarding me potentially going deaf one day. What was once something viewed as a work-around possibility became an overnight impossibility, and I was forced out of my position as a senior executive. Within three weeks of going deaf, I was suddenly out of work and on medical leave while waiting for my second pending brain surgery. I essentially had no further contact from any of the persons I worked with in the business world, many of whom just three weeks earlier were like family to me. Some of these relationships spanned over a decade. I was at an utter loss. Loss of job, income, friendships, responsibilities, and of course, my identity as a professional person hit me all at once.

The one person who has remained close to me from the days in business was also the only one of those friends to come visit me while I was in the hospital. Rick Jarrar was a beacon of light as a friend to me in those days. He was true and loyal, willing to help my wife and me with the most sincere attitude of "Anything you need at all, just ask." Although he no longer lives in the States, Rick and I still remain in contact. He, too, went through a similar experience of professional loss and abandonment, and so we've been able to be of encouragement to each another.

One of my favorite songs, with just some killer harmonies, was from another great band, Ambrosia. Their hit "Holding on to Yesterday," contained lyrics which are etched into my mind. The lyrics of the song describe the desire to hold on to the memories and experiences of the past. And I can tell you without any hesitation, that the words of this song title have continued to hold great meaning for me in recent years. The songs, the melodies, and the rhythms—I keep holding on to them. I have no desire to let go, as they were the core of who I was as a musician. They help bring sanity to the craziness of silence in my life when I find myself grieving the absence of music. Old church hymns and Top 40 songs alike, I keep holding on to what I can remember.

I guess that's yet another sense, or as I've come to believe, another God-given blessing to each of us—the gift of memory. Yeah, I still am like the dog with a bone in a lot of ways, holding on with a tight grip. Yet at the same time, I'm learning how to *hold on loosely* to the things in my life which I cannot keep, and those things that I choose to release in forgiveness.

Walk This Way

Back in the day when I was going to high school and in my early professional years of music, the band Aerosmith sure had the hits. It was hard to turn on the radio for more than an hour without hearing one of their tunes. As of 2011, Steven Tyler, the renowned front man whose vocals bring the matchless styles of soul and rock together, is a fresh and dominant force as a judge on *American Idol.*

Even with closed-captioning, I can't make it through a single episode of that show without hearing his voice in my head. What's odd to me is that I never purchased any of their albums when I was growing up. But I can tell you I loved their music and their unique style. It wasn't until I had already lost the ability to make out any sense of music that I actually went with my son to see a great show consisting of Mötley Crüe and Aerosmith together. What I missed out on musically at that concert, those boys made up for with effects and masterful showmanship. In my opinion, Steven is just in a league all by himself!

I decided to include some references to Steven Tyler and Aerosmith for a couple of purposes. The first being that even though I've been totally deaf for several years now, there are some real fond memories tucked deep away in my mind that I relive often. This is truly something I treasure immensely.

As I was writing this book and checking out various song titles from back in the day when I was a drummer, I found that as I was reading a specific song title, the song would jump right out in my mind. Sometimes, those songs would stay with me for days on end, and I would have to force myself to switch gears to something else. Like, I would tell myself, "Enough of this tune already." It's crazy how that works. Sometimes we don't give a whole lot of thought to the common everyday things in life, until they're a piece of the past that we so desperately need to identify with again.

The other reason I choose to write of Aerosmith was because of a truly funny story, which happened to me during a time I was really struggling with the challenges of being deaf. It was Christmastime and my wife Monica and I were in church on a Sunday morning, as usual. Each week as we attended church, I would try to understand as much of the message as possible by following along on the pastor's outline. For me, Monica is my interpreter for most situations outside of our home. So, as the musicians were playing a selection of songs, Monica turned toward me and spoke. I do pretty well with lipreading, especially with her. But what came out of her mouth just made me start laughing. You see, I thought she said, "Oh, I love this! This is one of my favorite Aerosmith songs." I looked at her, puzzled, while I was laughing and said, "What? What do you mean they're playing an Aerosmith song?"

She said, "Why are you talking about Aerosmith here in church? I said, 'This is one of my favorite Christmas songs.'" I don't know how I missed lipreading that one! All I could think about was, perhaps they were going to jam "Walk This Way" and then have the wise men come out on the stage as part of the Christmas theme going on that day. We still laugh about that story every time we talk about it.

I try my best to find the humor in life as often as possible. I mean, we all find tragedies of every sort around us. Sometimes, a few minutes of the nightly news or a few clicks on the Internet will provide more sorrowful tragedies than a person should have to digest for a few days. So, when funny stuff happens, I like to grab hold and hold on tight. I love to laugh, and I've decided to replace the disappointment and tears from loss of hearing and music, as well as other situations I face, with as much laughter and joy I can possibly gather.

Each of us will have different paths we'll journey on through life. Countless books have been written on the subject of personal journeys, so I won't attempt to fill the page with platitudes or preach at you. But, more than likely, we will all face many forks in the road over the course of our lifetimes. Sometimes we take off down a path only to realize later that perhaps we made an unwise decision. Other times, we look back and can reflect with gratefulness for having taken a step of faith and traveled the path of our conscience. I seem to come to forks in the road often. I try my best to choose the road which would ultimately bring glory and honor to God. I've come to understand it's a process, and each stride I take requires me to take a step of faith. When I close my eyes and ask for God's guidance with whatever I'm dealing with, I can often hear the words as a form of encouragement to me to *walk this way.*

I Love Music

I don't think I've ever met a single person who didn't love some type of music or another. Most people have a few favorites, be they jazz, rock, classical, or country. Of course, the list of styles of music these days is much broader than the ones I've just listed, but the point is, we all tend to love certain types of music. Music is one of life's greatest forms of artistic expression. From melodies of the heart to inspired words capturing the writer's thoughts, musical compositions in various forms have transcended generations and will continue to do so unabated.

In fact, oftentimes people gravitate toward other people who like the same types of music. Growing up, my best friends and I always shared the same love for music and enjoyed the same styles. I mean, if the musical tastes of two people were radically different, that could limit some aspects of their friendship, especially if music is often a part of their shared time together.

Music is a funny thing in that, for most people, the music you love most you play the loudest. You ever notice that? I mean, think about when you're driving down the road and a great tune is playing on your CD system or iPod. First thing most folks do is turn it up. The louder the better! I mean, give me the concert sound system in the car, and let's ride ... Am I right? How many times did you hear your parents tell you, "Turn that music down"? You loved it and you wanted to do more than just hear it, you wanted to "feel" it.

Music stirs our souls, and when we find a connection with a song, we want the total sensory involvement of hearing and feeling the song to resonate throughout our whole bodies. I'm not talking about music so loud it hurts one's ears, just right up to that threshold of pleasure before pain.

I have to tell you that I've loved many types of music over my lifetime. I switched back and forth over the years throughout my performance career depending on the bands I was with and the various styles I endeavored to master. Whether it was jazz, funk, rock, or R&B, I was on a never-ending mission to become the best I could in playing each of these styles. Although I must confess it was always R&B and funk I loved most. Take away all the new-hype names and labels of today, and the grooves still fall back to the core styles of early drumming.

For me to write that "I love music" is really an understatement. Even to this day, I find myself writing songs in my head, the lyrics along with the melodies. The challenge for a deaf musician is the inability to hear the creation beyond what's developed within the mind. For me, it's all there, all the various instrumentation and vocal parts with harmonies and all. But that's as far as I go with a song these days. The melody and lyrics are just locked away and never realized as a completed work.

I've had many people try to share encouraging words of "How cool it is to write tunes in your mind," yet in their most sincere expressions of support and encouragement, they don't fully understand just how frustrating it is to not to be able to complete the writing process. Not to be able to put it out in the air and hear it. Songs on paper or in the mind are incomplete until they are performed. That's where life is breathed into a melody and passion finds a lyric. It's where the two are joined together, and that relationship creates the opportunity for listeners to embrace the creation of the work. It's at that point that auditory senses are stimulated and minds kick into gear to fully appreciate a finished song. All of which makes us able to sit back and say, "*I love music!*"

Dizzy... My Head is Spinning

Do you remember being a kid and spinning around and around again until you fell over? I still see kids doing that at play. It might have been fun back then, but it's not so much fun now. Let me be real candid here, being dizzy to the point of falling over on a regular basis is nothing enjoyable.

It's funny in a peculiar sort of way how, without malice, so many medical procedures don't seem to come with a warning label. Sure, the doctors will tell you of the glaring risks; yet in my experience, the focus is on the rewards rather than the risks.

One of the permanent disabilities I incurred from my second surgery was the onset of severe vertigo. Now when I use the word "severe," I don't mean it in a trite sort of way. I mean it's a huge problem for me. I can't walk without a cane or I will literally fall over. When I stand up from being seated, I often fall back in the chair or down on the couch. It keeps me laughing with friends and family, but as I get older, it gets a little more painful when the fall happens on something not so soft and cushy.

Having talked at length with my neurologist, I've learned that the surgeries damaged my balance nerves on both sides, hence my ongoing challenges. On most days I end up having to take several breaks, and either sit or lie down to get the world to stop spinning so badly. Sometimes the dizziness will go away in thirty to sixty minutes. Often it is with me all day. So much so that frequently I will tell my wife I have to stop an activity because I feel sick to my stomach from being so dizzy. Although I have a couple of medicines to help with the dizziness, they pretty much knock me out, and then I find myself in a sleep mode for the rest of the day.

There's no telling what each day will bring. Some days I'm able to manage with my cane and occasionally bump into walls and other surfaces while navigating around my home or when we go out in public. Other days it's just a battle all day long. But isn't that how life is on every level? We never know what tomorrow will bring and all we can do is our best to stay the course each day and embrace the blessings of the moment.

So, when I see kids at play spinning themselves around, or I observe folks on amusement park rides going round and round at a stupid speed in order to become freakishly dizzy, well, I just gotta laugh! It's at that moment I realize I'm saving a whole bunch of money for myself because I've already got that for free. It sure brings the old saying to mind, "Be careful what you wish for because you might just get it." Can't help but think that maybe one of my wishes as a young child after spinning myself dizzy was, "I wish I could feel like this all the time!"

As I was working on a subtitle for this book, one of the words I chose with great purpose was "journey." Although the meaning applies to the better part of my story, it physically has no greater significance than how it relates to me trying to walk. One of the definitions of the word *journey* is described as, "an act of traveling from one place to another."[2] Without exception, I have to preplan my every step. It doesn't matter if I'm going from one room another, I have to look ahead and consciously plan out my route. I never thought in my life I'd have to actually calculate my every step and then either lean on my cane or use the furniture and walls to balance myself just to walk a few feet. All this simply from being so *dizzy* ... that *my head is spinning.*

---

2 Dictionary App. New Oxford American Dictionary Second Edition 2005 by Oxford University Press, Inc.

Communication Breakdown

Yeah, I told you I had a wide variety of musical interests back in the day. Now, I know for some of you reading these song titles and then thinking about the groups who recorded them, you might be thinking, "Hey Tim, you listened to some pretty hardcore groups, and their lifestyles were as colorful and descriptive as anything out there." Well, yes, you're correct about that, and I'm not proud of the fact that I spent so many hundreds of hours saturating my mind with such lyrics. In point of fact, I wish I would have known more about the lyrics, rather than just focusing on the music. Although I was a master of being able to focus on just the drums or other instruments I was concentrating on to study the specific parts, there is no way to completely "mute" the lyrics being sung.

Unfortunately for me, that translated into hundreds (and most likely thousands) of hours of my mind being subject to vast numbers of lyrics that were totally contrary to biblical teachings. What's so hard for me to grasp, even to this day, is just how much crap (yeah, that's the best word for it that I can think of) I listened to over and over again, just to learn and memorize what the drummer was playing. It's only recently, since becoming deaf, that I often will catch some of these songs on various television music specials and then read the actual lyrics by means of closed-captioning. Wow, I'm amazed at what a lot of those songs were actually about.

Music has always been a form of free speech in this country, and a lot of times artists capitalize on using controversial words and metaphors to promote their artistic endeavors. Well, before the day of posting explicit lyric ratings on published musical works, the lyrics still contained explicit content. Part of the issue was a breakdown in communication. Many people turned a "deaf ear" to the groups whose songs had the most demeaning and vulgar lyrics because, quite simply, they just chose not to listen to the stuff. My folks were no different. Their idea of governing what I listened to in my musical selections was simply, "Timmy, turn that down."

I was five years old when I first heard The Beatles and bought my first Beatles record right after. I wore that record out dancing to "I Wanna Hold Your Hand." I even won a dance contest doing the Twist, dancing with a teenage girl to that song. Man, that music just stirred my soul, and I loved their songs. I didn't know anything about lyrics and content. I just loved the music, and it beat the heck out of listening to what my folks listened to in those days (or any other time, for that matter).

After all those years in music, thousands of hours of listening, practicing, performing, and recording, it's only after I went deaf that I really started to focus on and follow what the heck vocalists were singing. Something I often tell people these days in all sincerity is, "I hear more now, being deaf, then I did when I could hear."

I've come to realize that hearing has nothing to do with listening. I learned this truth from the Bible. There are several references to people having ears but not hearing. In other words, just because someone has the ability to hear something doesn't mean he or she is listening.

Being deaf has forced me to become a better listener. I always thought being really good at listening to that which I focused upon was a strength for me. And it was. Yet at times, I know I would turn a "deaf ear" toward conversations—"check out" so to speak, by not paying attention. I took several communication courses over the years, and the phrase "active listening" was often used in them to describe effective communication with other people. This was accomplished by getting feedback from the other person, verifying that you actually heard what they were trying to communicate.

Since I'm nowhere near proficient at sign language, and the majority of the time I am around friends who do not know how to sign, I've had to learn to speechread in order to engage in any sort of basic dialogue. Even then, I have to frequently ask my wife to help me in conversations with those around me. Some of the time, my family and close friends have to repeat themselves, sometimes three and four times, before I get what they are trying to communicate to me. They will say a sentence and then I will try to repeat back what they just said to me. Sometimes I get it the first time, and a lot of times we end up making multiple attempts before the communication is complete.

Over and over the words are spoken until I get it right. What would normally take only a few seconds for someone to speak and another person to hear can take several minutes with me. It's frustrating for me to have to ask people to repeat themselves over and over again, not to mention physically exhausting for me to try to focus my vision to lipread what the heck they're saying! Then there is the patience required on their part in trying to talk to this deaf guy ... Oh, it can be so exasperating for everyone involved, just to try to exchange a few basic sentences.

I've been so blessed over these recent years to have some very supportive and loving friends who display such tolerance and support to me in their willingness to communicate with me. For years, I had a dear friend named Julia Dinwiddie who would come to church each week and type out for me what the pastor was preaching. She would bring her laptop and stenograph machine just so I could keep up with the church service. These days, I'm fortunate enough that the pastor sends me his notes so I can try to follow along. I struggle to focus my vision for more than ten minutes or so at a time. Then I have to take a break and pick up again. Luckily, our pastor takes frequent side trips from his notes, so I get the break. By the end of the church service, I'm worn out and just want to close my eyes for a while.

That's the way life is for me these days. I've really had to learn to pace myself with people and conversations. I have to take a lot of long breaks throughout the day when trying to read closed-captions on television or reading in general. It's frustrating to not be able to keep up. Yet I'm grateful for having the ability to rest as often as I need. Often, my day consists of a couple of naps, coupled with long breaks almost every hour just to rest my eyes.

While working on this chapter, I came to understand through personal study a great truth that has helped me gain new perspective and helps me deal with the ongoing challenges in both communication and with life in general. That is, learning the difference between being patient and long-suffering. I used to use these words interchangeably without giving much thought to their original meaning. I discovered that being patient about my circumstances is something I should strive toward— patience to endure the process, so to speak. Allowing enough time for the circumstances to run their course. Being long-suffering is what I must try to demonstrate toward individuals. I like to think of this in biblical terms as being quick to love and forgive, slow to anger, slow to speak and eager to listen. For me, learning to separate the two and purposefully working toward applying these practices has been of tremendous value.

The reality of my condition forces me to go slowly, to be patient, and to just try to get through each day, one day at a time. Yet with new insight, I've developed a far greater appreciation and depth of gratitude for those willing to be patient with my circumstances and long-suffering toward me as a person. Don't mistake what I'm writing here, for this is no easy process. It takes work! And I mean a lot of work and from everyone involved. Yet the investment of both time and energy is more than worth it! Otherwise, my days would end up frustrating and disappointing as a result of a total *communication breakdown.*

We Can Work It Out

This was one of my all-time favorite tunes. I'm talking about the song originally written by Paul McCartney and John Lennon and, of course, recorded and released by The Beatles in 1965. I was just about to turn seven years old when that song was first played on the radio. I already had one Beatles album and, believe it or not, I was a huge fan at that age. I mean, my mom and dad were in the late thirties when I was born, and all they listened to was "old folks" music.

Out of the blue, along came The Beatles, and my musical pallet of rhythms was forever changed. Yep, I loved this song right out of the gate. I'll admit I was way too young to have any sort of understanding about its message, but the tune was great and I loved to dance to every fast song The Beatles wrote.

Now, if you look at the list of artists who have taken that song and done their own cover version, you would hopefully find yourself inspired by many musicians who loved that tune just like I did. Stevie Wonder did my favorite version, without exception. By the time

Stevie recorded this song, the lyrics made sense, and when I sang along, it felt way more personal than back in those first days when I was a young kid.

In a nutshell, the song's lyrics are about two people not understanding each other. Each one is trying to get their personal view across to the other, and then, realizing if they both remain stubborn, they may have a falling out and end their friendship.

As I was writing this chapter, those lyrics hit me with far greater impact than ever before. Often, it seems when I'm trying to share with others my frustrations of missing out on what's being communicated and going on around me, I feel as though they don't "hear" me. As I wrote earlier, I can be in a crowded room and yet feel alone just from not being a part of a conversation or not being able to listen in on what people are saying.

Those times of being unable to participate in the conversation frequently lead me to feel sad or defeated. In those situations, when I'm feeling totally vexed, I'll interrupt folks and blurt out, "What? What are you guys talking about?" Internally, I routinely have to restrain myself, because what I really want to say is, "Hey, a little help here! Can you folks throw some words my way and bring me up to speed?"

I generally give casual acquaintances a lot of grace for not realizing my limitations. Yet I sometimes have more difficulty being long-suffering toward those who know my situation well and forget to include me. Usually, they can tell when I'm feeling that way, but every once in a while, they will get so involved in their own conversations without taking a break to clue me in that I will jump in and ask, "What are you all talking about?"

But that's the easier part of the process of working it out. When it comes to people getting upset with one another and tempers beginning to elevate, or a topic becomes heated, that makes things really tough for me. You see, I can see the total change in their facial expressions and body language, and that's what hits me first. But then, there's the added element of what the majority of people do when topics are backed with emotion and passion—they talk faster and louder. Not that the "louder" matters to me at all ...

So picture that in your mind for a minute. Your family or dear friends are in a heated conversation, and all you can do is try to catch a word here and there while trying to speechread someone's lips from the side of their face. After all, since I'm not in the conversation, they aren't looking at me whatsoever. That's a double complexity added to the mix.

Recently, my wife and I were dealing with some family-related issues and we felt the persons involved and their actions were very disrespectful toward us. I started off with some questions such as, "Why would you do that without asking us?" Suddenly, the individual's response became very agitated, and he began walking up toward me. My wife jumped in and expressed her frustration, and before I knew it, the person was having words with her.

Now, let me interject something here for background purposes. In my early years, in between music and working at the shipyard for my father, I used to get hired as a bouncer at local clubs. The first thing I learned from lead bouncers and friends who were bodyguards, the peacekeepers of events, was to step in between the arguing parties and defuse the situation before a physical altercation ensued. With that in mind, let me get back to the family confrontation.

During the course of the argument, as this individual shifted his focus from me to my wife, something clicked in me; I'm just saying, I wasn't about to allow him to get in my wife's face. The weird part in all this for me was that I knew the questions I was asking and what I was saying, but I didn't have a clue about what anyone else was talking about. After a few exchanges of what I perceived to be a lot of ranting and increased volume, we finally calmed down. We didn't get to a point of yelling or name-calling (I know this because I asked my wife about that very thing), but we were sure standing close to that tipping point—just a few degrees shy of boiling.

As you may have noticed in my writing style, I'm a very passionate person and my emotions often run very high. This is especially true with those whom I love, like my family and closest friends.

Like the song lyrics from the title of this chapter, I totally wanted the other people in this situation to see things my way. My wife and I felt violated and utterly disrespected as a result of that person's actions. Of course, on the other side, they felt justified in their course of action. In the sixty minutes following that initial confrontation, we arrived at a place where we exchanged mutual apologies and hugged before departing. Yet I've got to tell you, it was sure difficult at best to be in the middle of a situation and wanting to defend my wife while being totally left out of the exchange of words.

Now, I'm not trying to teach a lesson here about forgiveness or how to have a proper argument nor anything about conflict resolution. I'm just saying that I used to take for granted the ability to have a good old-fashioned battle of opinions without even realizing the blessing of having been able to hear all of the heated conversation in the first place.

Kids yelling, dogs barking late in the night, people laying on their horns while driving in traffic and so on and so on ... Some days, I'd just love to hear all that again, as it would mean I'd be able to hear everything else I miss so greatly. I'm sure there are a number of people who would think it would be great to not have to hear all of the junk in life. But hey! You have to take the bad with the good, and it's only when you no longer have either, that you realize just how much you would give to get it all back.

I'll never hear again, at least not until I get to heaven. But in the meantime, in the midst of all the turmoil and my frustrations of not being able to understand what others always say or wondering if they're hearing me, one thing remains of constant encouragement: with a willingness to honor and be patient with each other, no matter what the circumstance, objection, or issue is, *we can work it out.*

Stairway to Heaven or a Highway to Hell

So many songs have been written about the predominant question of which direction you are heading. Many lyrics cause us to reflect on the journey of life and the destination we're heading toward.

For the greater part of my life, I endeavored to be a faithful follower of Christ Jesus. Yet, with all honesty, I must tell you that I've sure had my share of falling off the path of righteousness and stumbling through the thicket of the weeds and thorns of temptation. Most of the other musicians I hung out with seemed to share many of the same challenges that I did—sex, drugs, alcohol, and prideful egos. Within that music scene, what made the major difference for me was the way in which I was raised.

My mother instilled in me a reverence, a holy fear of God and taught me to respect the words of God found in the Bible; she left me a deep sense of moral values and ethics. The problem for me was that during my years as a musician, I was more focused on what I wanted to do in life, rather than what God wanted me to do. I was way more interested in my fame and glory than His. That's not me preaching at you, that's just the fact of the matter.

In hopes of bringing words of encouragement, I want to be completely transparent with you. Although I would like to think I've always been on the *stairway to heaven,* taking steps toward a more purposed and intimate relationship with God, the reality is that's just not always been true in my life. You see, truth be told here, instead of that stairway, my life choices and actions were leading me down a *highway to hell.* As a Christian and believer that Jesus Christ is the Son of God, I fundamentally knew my salvation couldn't be stripped away. Nonetheless, I was dangerously racing toward potentially hellish consequences.

At age forty-eight, I found myself out of control and lost. I was deaf and unemployed. Let me create a bit of a mental picture for you to help illustrate one of the most unpleasant periods in my life. Have you ever been on a two-lane highway and flying down the asphalt at seventy miles per hour? If you have, you know the road markers and turn off signs come up pretty quick. I've driven all kinds of these roads throughout the country, and when the signs say, "last gas for umpteen miles," they mean it. Sometimes you can take one of those exits and, if you didn't read the sign that told you which direction to take when you got to the stop sign, you could be in for a little "off the beaten path" experience. You may venture several miles off the main highway before you realize you done went and blew it.

Well, there I was and I was so out of control, I knew what the signs were warning me, but I didn't care and I didn't pay attention.

The first wrong turn I made was down the road of Despair.

I was feeling utterly hopeless in all areas of my life. Physically, spiritually, emotionally, and financially, I was devastated. I suddenly found myself unable to work and on permanent disability because of my two brain surgeries, the resulting deafness, and numerous physical side effects. I was without any leadership position as a professional, and much of who I was, my identity in life, was stripped away. One by one, everything in my life began to unravel.

Thinking I could drive myself out of my situation, in my stubbornness I continued on and before I knew it, I found myself traveling down the road with Depression.

I mean to tell you, depression was upon me before I knew it and hit me like a ton of bricks. Panic and anxiety attacks, cold sweats, trouble sleeping, and eating disorders were all part of depression's miserable family. They all came upon me and seemed to jump in the car, and I felt like there was no way of getting rid of the passengers that were now surrounding me. I thought they'd never leave. It was more than I could bear at times, and it led me to the point where I no longer cared if I lived or died. Though not suicidal in my thoughts, I was just hopelessly indifferent.

The best way to describe the state of mind I was operating under was being in a perpetual state of fog. Nothing helps when you're driving in a dense fog. You can't see the landscape around you, nor can you make out the warning signs along the way. Many people just keep plowing through, waiting for the fog to lift. That was me for sure, but by the time the fog had lifted, I had taken yet another wrong turn and was now venturing down the avenue of Desperation.

My feelings of indifference were most prevalent toward those closest to me. I felt so stripped of everything in my life that all I could feel was a huge void. It was nothing I'd ever experienced before, and the need to eradicate the utter emptiness I felt was all-consuming. The only thing I could focus on during my waking hours was trying to find something to make me feel alive again. Something which would give me back my passion in life. I was searching for some type of direction in order to get on the right road again. But I was so far out and heading toward the wrong destination that I was completely lost. I mean, I was utterly lost and without a GPS. I was desperate to eradicate the sorrow, pain, and isolation I was feeling each and every day. Something, anything to replace the emptiness I had inside.

You know, I should have just stopped and asked for directions. But no! Not me. In all my emptiness, I still had too much pride to admit I had a serious problem and was lost in life. Pride and arrogance is a lethal combination when it comes to having godly character. They can't coexist, as I was about to discover. I should have given more thought to the truth of the well-established saying that "character leads to conduct." I was totally blind to the fact that my desires were beginning to lead me toward that which I was about to do. Yeah, there I was, determined and desperate, trying to navigate my way out of depression and despair. My journey filled with one wrong turn after another wasn't quite over yet.

All the wrong turns led me to a place I hope to never visit again. When the fog had lifted, I found myself smack in the middle of a town called Distortion. It was there that I began to lose all godly perspective in life, and what I once was able to determine as areas of black and white moral clarity, suddenly became one big cloud of gray. I began to question my values. I found myself wanting, at any cost, to satisfy the longing for filling my emptiness. Trying to justify my behavior through rationalization, I kept telling myself, "Hey, I could be doing worse things in life." Well, with that kind of attitude and perspective, it didn't take me long to walk down the old sidewalks of the town of Distortion and venture into a most historic landmark that many come to visit and some never leave.

It was alluring from the outside, and the temptation to enter was more than I could fight off on my own. Like the old western saloons with the double doors, I pushed through and walked straight into the parlor of Disobedience.

Suddenly, I found myself beginning to justify my actions by comparing them to the opportunity for making worse choices. I qualified my behavior by telling myself, "As long as I'm not hurting anybody else, then it's no big deal." I stepped down so far as to try to sell myself on the idea that *I know what I'm doing is wrong, but God will forgive me.* That's true and I knew it, but I was so misguided and lost in my direction that I didn't bother to take notice that I had become all too comfortable residing in that place of Disobedience. As a result of my flagrant behavior, I never considered that housed next door to Disobedience was a place called Dependency.

I was so far from the road I once turned off. The title of the song, "Highway to Hell" should have told me it wasn't a slow methodical journey, which would allow for frequent U-turns to get back on the right road in life. Nope. I should have paid a lot more attention and realized that the Highway to Hell is also the expressway to all kinds of evils.

What once started out as a little side trip suddenly turned into a nine-month trip of denial and derailment! When I finally discovered where I had ended up, the consequences left me feeling completely Distant and Detached from God, my family, and my friends.

I was completely detached from the values and priorities I once held with great conviction. I had distanced myself from several long-time, treasured friendships. I became detached from my church. I had become distant from my children and my wife. I had allowed myself to detach emotionally from those who loved me most. I even went so far as to distance myself from God. Previously in my life, I would have never imagined embarking on such a journey.

There are many specifics I could share with you regarding my choice of void-fillers during that most dreadful period. Some of them have left me with great remorse. One story serves to show the depths I went to fill the emptiness in my life. Prior to delving into the specific details, I must clarify that I do suffer from obsessive-compulsive behavior. This is a common problem for people like me who also struggle with clinical depression. This might help you understand why my actions were so obsessive.

Well, enough of that. Here it goes:

Within a nine-month period, I purchased over seventy pairs of athletic shoes. Yeah, that's correct, seventy—70—pairs. To go along with my collection of shoes, I also bought forty warm-up suits. To complete my attire, I just had to have thirty matching baseball hats.

I would purchase something on the Internet and feel completely productive that day. If it was on sale, then I felt as though it was an even bigger success. I became friends with a local manager at an athletic store, and soon I was able to make purchases at forty, and sometimes fifty percent off the normal price. I never had to wait for a sale. Oh, I was addicted to shopping and I had a supplier. You put that combination into the hands of someone who is obsessive-compulsive and it can become catastrophic. I was completely out of control. My wife and children stood by helplessly as I obsessively tried to fill the hole in my heart ... and the packages continued to arrive.

Then, out of the blue, something profound happened to me one day that I can only describe as a time where God revealed to me what I needed to learn about myself. He showed me I had all those pairs of shoes, yet I didn't have any direction in my steps. I had all those hats to cover my head, yet I was empty in my thinking. All those clothes I had purchased were the result of my feeble attempts to cover up my anguish and loneliness. Loud and clear He made it plain to me that I had stuffed away my Christ-centered compass and refused to seek direction.

Several months later, I ended up giving away a lot of the clothes and shoes I had purchased—things I had thought I just *had* to have. I can tell you, I hope and pray to never travel down that highway again. What was once too painful to talk about has now become a focal point of my life's message. I hope my story can be a road sign to those who are on that lonely freeway of self-destruction, speeding down that *highway to hell,* to pull off and not continue to venture on all those dreadful roads. My greatest desire is that my testimony will inspire you to choose a new route, one with purposed steps upon the *stairway to heaven.*

Lessons in Love

Something about experiencing the gravest circumstances in life makes our loved ones often become even dearer to us. I can't begin to fathom going through two brain surgeries, the arduous periods of recovery, and the ongoing challenges of each day without my wife beside me.

Although my faith in God is my ultimate source of steadfast encouragement and hope, I truly believe God has chosen to reveal His love for me through the actions of my wife and children. No husband or father could ever have asked for greater support than that I've received and continue to receive from my family.

Now, I'm not saying we haven't hit a few potholes in the road, because we have. But truth be told, those holes in the pavement were in plain sight, and I took my eyes of the road and ran straight over them. Almost in a form of arrogance, feeling like "I've made it through three major surgeries in my life, a nine-hour back surgery, and two nine-plus hour brain surgeries, and I can conquer anything."

Well, I was wrong. Real wrong. I mean, stupidly arrogant and foolishly wrong. Are you with me on how wrong I was?

That's where I believe God wanted to teach me about some lessons in love. After my little excursion down the Highway of Hell, I discovered the reality of having to face myself in the mirror and attempt to do so with integrity. As a result, I realized there was much for me to learn. I had to gain the knowledge that no distance or speed could take me beyond the boundaries of God's limitless love.

This was also a time for me to witness the heartache I had created for my wife and the concern I was causing our children. "What's going on with Dad? Is he going to be okay?" were questions they thought about often and asked as frequently. And let me say that uncertainty is not a positive characteristic in a father figure. A father needs to display steadfastness and commitment to his family, to his wife and his children, and I had failed to do this at that point in my life.

Yet in the midst of the chaos, God was in control. He would hear and answer the requests and countless prayers of family and dear friends. His answer came through the patience and persistence of my wife as she continued to love me with unswerving devotion. Seeing her and the heartache I was causing her forced me to come to grips with the road of destruction I was traveling. It was in her obedience to God that He chose to speak in my life. It was through her examples of love that I felt her love and the love of a merciful God, which helped me get turned around and back on the right road.

At no point in my life have I ever gained greater wisdom from such real-life lessons. This period was filled with unmatched true-life applications, which can't be expressed or learned through a textbook or course of study. Most assuredly, they can't be assimilated by watching some reality TV show. I believe some lessons just need to be experienced in real life through real situations. You know, the kind of personal and upfront in-your-face types of life lessons. That's what the majority of this book is all about.

When I think back to those days of my deepest trials and reflect upon the unconditional love of God, which saw me through, I am so grateful! When I pause to look at my wife, and think about all her heart endured, I am continually moved to tears. For most of my life, people have told me I am a passionate person. Yet with all that passion, I had a lot to learn, and that's when I was taught some of my life's most meaningful lessons. Lessons about truth, commitment, honor and selflessness. All of which I most desperately needed to learn again. These most profound times would restore my heart of passion, and teach me those *lessons in love.*"

So Much More in Love

You may not have ever heard this song. I kind of doubt you have, but it holds such a powerful story. You see, I wrote this song for my wife. It was on an album I recorded with a great friend of mine at that time, Lamon Davis. We had formed our own music act and called ourselves Excalibur. When we produced the album—yeah, album, not CD—the album cover was a photo of a white Excalibur car, and the model sitting on the car was my wife. In fact, she was a couple months pregnant with our son at the time, but you'd never be able to notice because she was simply stunning. Not the car, my wife! So much so, that we used those exact words, "Simply Stunning" as the title for our album.

Now, back to the song and the meaning behind it. A couple of great friends of mine, who happen to be brothers, Scott and Sam Baris, owned and operated several young adult nightclubs. They were, for the most part, just like any nightclub, with one exception: they didn't serve any alcohol. The lights and sound systems were the most advanced anywhere, and these clubs could pack in several hundred people, ages seventeen and up.

At the time, I was in one of San Diego's best known eight piece bands, Higher Ground. We had a killer rhythm structure and equally powerful horn section. Our lead vocalist, Lee Daniels, and bass player, Ed Graves (who also did lead vocals), were great friends of mine for many years. Both of them had the amazing talent of being able to sound like the respective vocalists from the top Billboard artists' songs we performed. We played some of the most difficult cover tunes any band could perform in those days. Very few bands could pull off playing songs from Tower of Power, Chicago, Steely Dan, Average White Band, and Earth, Wind & Fire the way we did. It was one of the best cover bands I ever performed with as a drummer. Needless to say, we had a very large following of people who loved those groups.

It was at one of our shows at these young adult nightclubs that Monica came to see us perform. She was just as sweet and cute as could be. Not just good-looking, mind you, but she had just a real sincere and sweet disposition, and there was just something very different about her compared to all the other girls I knew in high school and from playing clubs.

We started dating on a regular basis and did so for a while. She gave me a picture of herself that she had taken by a professional photographer, and that was a first for me. No girl I ever dated had given me a photo to keep. But when summer ended and she had to continue on in school, the drive for us was a bit far to keep seeing each other a few times a week. We just kind of drifted apart, and then one day I got a call to go on tour with a very successful band at that time, The Steppin Stones. Monica ended up with another high school boyfriend for several years, but we kept in touch and I kept her photo with me. In fact, I kept it on my nightstand and never took it down.

Over four years went by, and I was then drumming for a new band. I was the last person to join the group, and they were working on a recording project and had some concert dates set up. The band was called Legend and was comprised of some truly talented songwriters and musicians. Our band's producer, Clarence McDonald, was without exception the most amazing musician and producer I've ever had the privilege of working with. His musical credits and accomplishments in the music industry read like a Who's Who. Clarence was someone who invested a lot of time into my life, affirming my abilities and talents, and as a result, the things he shared helped me tremendously in my ensuing musical endeavors.

Well, it was late one evening, and I had just gotten out of a rehearsal for an upcoming concert we had scheduled. I decided to head over to a nearby record store on my way home to pick up a new album some friends had just released. After buying the album, I was walking out to get in my car and I heard a young woman's voice call my name. "Tim? Tim, is that you?" I looked and saw this incredibly beautiful lady sitting in her car and, after a second or two, I recognized who it was. It was Monica! Wow, I could hardly believe it. It had been several years since I'd seen her, and she was even more amazing-looking than the last time.

I walked up to her and we started talking about this and that. You know, "How are you?", "What have you been up to?", and so on. I'm sure most of my side of the conversation was me being an idiot, because all I could think of was to ask if she still had the same boyfriend or not? You see, I wanted to cut right to the chase and see if she was available. So, I guess perhaps ten minutes or so passed, and then I just had to ask, "Are you still dating the same guy?"

She replied, "No." So, of course, I had to do the follow-up to that one: "Well, are you dating anyone right now?"

And she said, "No." Yeah baby, I was in. No boyfriend and I was active and on the scene.

I was so nervous, I was afraid to ask her out right then. So, since she had just told me she was a hairstylist, I thought "Perfect."

"Can I get the number to the salon where you work so I can make an appointment to have you cut my hair?" Guess what? It worked! I got her new phone number and the next day I called. She had an opening that very day, and so I headed right over to get my haircut. Funny thing is, I had just gotten it cut the week before, but hey, it's hair and it grows, and I thought it was time to get it cut again (Yeah, right!). So, there I was getting my hair washed and cut by my old girlfriend, and she was just amazing to be around again. Just as she was finishing up with the last few snips, I managed to work up the courage to ask her if she would like to go out with me sometime. She said sure, but she was leaving the following day to go to Hawaii for a week and would get back just before the Fourth of July.

That sure seemed like a long week for me. I was so excited to go out with her. She mailed me a postcard from Hawaii and that just made my day. When she got back it was a Sunday and I called her. We talked for hours about her trip. Finally, I worked up the nerve again to ask if she wanted to go out that night to get dinner and see a movie. She did, and so I took her to a really good little Chinese place and ordered the best things I could think of. When the food came, I couldn't eat a bite. I mean, this girl had me captivated and I just didn't feel hungry a bit. We then went to see the movie *E.T.* The whole night, all I could do was keep looking at her. There was just something tugging at my heart from the first moment I saw her again and she just completely got me all twisted up inside.

From that night of our date, we went out every single night but one for three months straight. After those three months, I knew she was the only one for me and so I asked her to marry me. Six months later, we were married and we just celebrated our twenty-ninth anniversary.

Now, about that song "So Much More in Love." Well, it's a love ballad I wrote for her and it tells our story of how we once dated and then grew apart. How I kept her picture by my bedside hoping we would meet again. How our paths did cross and we began dating and fell in love. But this time, we were older and so much more in love than ever before.

When I wrote about heading down the Highway to Hell, I was describing a specific time in my life, the only time I can ever recall where I didn't have passion or feelings of being in love. To tell you that Monica was so patient and loving with me in trying to understand all I was going through would be an understatement. No words could ever justly paint the picture of how she remained steadfast in her love and devotion to God and to me, at a time where I was utterly numb.

A few months had gone by with me being in that awful state, that horrible frame of mind, and so we decided what we needed was to take a vacation. Sometimes in the midst of the storm, you've just got to try and find a break, some smooth waters so to speak. We ended up going to Puerto Vallarta for a week; suddenly, within a few days or our being there, it was like running into her at the record store all over again.

I found myself being filled with feelings of love once again. Love for God, my wife, and our children. Once again, I began to feel impassioned, and it was as if a huge weight was removed from my chest. During those few months, my heart had become closed down and guarded in my attempts to "tough out" all of the physical and emotional pain I was dealing with. Yet God heard the prayers of a broken heart, and His answer didn't come in the form of a temporary repair. You see, still to this day, each time I look at

Monica or hold her hand and look into her beautiful blue eyes, my heart overflows with the feeling of being *so much more in love.*

Enjoy the Silence

Years ago when I first became totally deaf, I was facing a whole set of overwhelming situations. Many of those I still face today. They are still just as challenging to me, but now I face them with gained perspective and have worked through several strategies to cope with them on a daily basis.

During the first couple of months of my deafness, I discovered a brief quote which really had quite an impact on me. You know how sometimes you can come across something that hits you at a point in your life where it becomes a personal revelation to you? Well, that's what happened to me one morning when I was reading a devotional book. It impacted me so much that I grabbed my journal and started writing. It still holds tremendous relevance for me today, and I trust it will inspire you as well.

"There is no music in a rest, but there is the making of music in it."[3]
—John Ruskin

3 Quote from Life's Rests by John Ruskin 1819-1900

As I began writing my own thoughts about this statement, I couldn't help but reflect upon my relationship with God and gave significant thought towards these words as they related to my faith and my life. After all, the two go hand in hand for me. So, with pen and paper in hand, I wrote the following:

"In the symphony of our lives, the melody consists of rests within the measures of the manuscript. Sometimes, God will send to us forced times of rest. Sometimes it's through sickness, or plans that didn't go as we dreamed or planned out for ourselves. It's at times like these that we often will exclaim our frustrations and cry out to God; at other times we have to be silent."

As a musician for the greater part of my life, one thing I can tell you for sure is this: not every instrument in the symphony, nor every member of the choir, can always be playing or singing at the same volume or at all times. Otherwise, it would be dull and nothing more than chaos, lapping over and overpowering noise.

Regardless of an individual's musical talent, when it comes to writing music, there is a fundamental key involved in the art of composing any great musical work. That is, to know how to let the composition "breathe." Whether classical or hip-hop, metal or jazz, all great songs have one common element, and that is to let the song breathe and develop. Be it through the building of the music or the hook of the lyrics, they all take us someplace and leave us wanting more. Yet it is that rest in the measure and that forced breath which is fundamental to create. It takes discipline and skill as well as a willingness to lay back and let the song flow.

As the Composer and Conductor of each of our life's symphonies, God knows the entire piece, every measure, note by note. Although we may find the desire to improvise and "jam a little" to show our creative "licks," God ultimately desires for us to return to His composition. After all, that's where faith and trust go hand in hand. Doing this is something I still work through on a daily basis.

That same day I wrote those words, I read a compelling verse from the Bible to support this principle, and it came from the Book of Psalms. I turned to Psalm 46:10, and it was as though God Himself had me turn to this exact passage, where I found the words, "Be still and know that I am God..."[4] There they were, the very words inspired from God, recorded for me to read.

Now this psalm was not new to me. As a matter fact, I had used this verse as the basis for one of the worship songs I wrote and recorded just before losing the ability to ever hear music again. Yet suddenly the words held such a fresh and new perspective for me. I had missed something in the depth of their meaning as it related to "being still" or being able to rest in the measures of the music. You see, I needed to learn how to relax and be willing to follow the music, one measure at a time. And with even greater significance, I had to come to grips with the fact that God is much more than just the conductor of this piece; He is the composer as well.

What an incredible time that was for me. I still have to remind myself often to trust God as the both the conductor and composer of my life and understand that He sets the tempo.

So much has changed from when I was actively involved in music. These days, I seem to be in a long series of "measures of rests," just like a percussionist playing the tympani drum. For a couple of years in high school, I was involved in the orchestra. Along with playing the snare drum, I also knew how to play the tympani drums. Sometimes, the difficulty in playing those parts is not the notes that are written, but rather the counting of the measures of rest and following along. It takes incredible focus and discipline to read music and count blank measures of rest, so at the

4 New king James Version

exact moment in the symphonic piece, the tympani will ring out with great force and make its unique contribution.

I've got to tell you, when I first came across the song title for this chapter, it didn't hit me at first. But then I thought about it, and the message still holds truth. In the song of our life, we all need to be able to understand the various aspects of the composition and above all, when the time comes for us to rest and follow along with the measures within the music, we need to learn how to *enjoy the silence.*

Silent Night

For over twenty-two years, some of the greatest music to my ears was that of the voices of my wife and children. This was especially true during the evenings.

From the days of our children's births and all through middle school, each evening would always end with talking together and praying before they went to sleep. As they grew, so did the challenges in their world, be it from school projects, the influence of friends, or various forms of peer pressure. The one constant routine we always believed in, and still do to this day, is the power of prayer with one another.

For over fifteen years of my life, this conscious commitment to prayer with our children at bedtime was a nightly occurrence. From singing Bible songs with them, to them sharing their fears and concerns, it was in their bedrooms with only a night-light on that forever etched those scenes into my memory.

Yet as sweet as those memories are even to this day, a deep-seated sadness clings to me. One which I believe I'll never be able to fully overcome. It was in the last moments of each day, when my wife and I would lie in bed with the lights out and the house quiet, that we would complete the day with conversation and prayer for our family and friends. Sometimes those moments would last only a few minutes, while other times we would carry on for the better part of an hour. Sometimes we would be overwhelmed with heavy hearts for the burdens of those we love. Other times, we would laugh and tell jokes to each other that we had been unable to do during the busier part of the evening.

It was there in the midst of the darkness, with my love beside me, that the day's end was always drawn to a close with the sound of her amazing tender voice. We never went to sleep angry, and so the last sounds I would hear are those that I miss most today. Even when I was traveling on business for several days at a time, each night ended as it did at home, with our talking on the phone, there in the dark as we lay in bed.

Being deaf changes those tender moments far beyond what most can comprehend. Today what I experience, when the lights are off, are the sounds of silence lingering there in the dark. When I cannot see her face, there are no conversations, no telling jokes, no last-minute reminders to discuss, not even the words, "I love you, goodnight." What once was the day's highlight has now significantly changed, for the sweet sound of my loved ones voices has been replaced with a piercing *silent night*.

I know I used to totally take for granted the ability to lie there in the dark, during the last moments between being awake and asleep. I now realize a most profound aspect in bringing closure to the day is found not in the stillness or silence, but in hearing the voices of those you love most dearly, before you slip away into slumber.

Friends

The first time I ever heard the song "Friends" by Michael W. Smith I was not so thrilled with it. It was a nice slow song with a good melody, but I wasn't much into playing ballads as a drummer because they are just boring most of the time to sit and play. At least that's how I felt about most of the slower songs back at that time in my life.

But as I grew up and matured both as a man and a musician, I became a huge fan of this particular song. Beyond the melody being one that just plain sticks with you, Deborah D. Smith wrote some of the most amazing lyrics about friendship I have ever come to read and sing along with whenever I would play the song.

The point, which has penetrated my heart in this song, is a simple message: that a relationship shared between friends, true friends, shouldn't fade away. The song passionately illustrates that the length of one's life is not too long to share in a mutual deep friendship. I've sung that song in my head so many times over the years. I wish I could tell both Michael and Deborah just how much their words and music have blessed me.

My mother passed away on December 22, 2009 at the age of eighty-nine. She was a godly woman and, I can tell you, that she wore out her knees praying for me. She pounded the gates of heaven with ongoing prayer petitions for my protection and that of my family. It was at her memorial service, when I had the opportunity to share, that I read the lyrics of this song and then proceeded to encourage all of the people paying tribute to my mother to live as friends.

My mother had a couple of very dear friends and their friendships spanned over fifty years. They were faithful and committed through the ups and downs of life. Through thick and thin, they never gave up on each other. My mother was the spiritual driving force in our home and she exemplified what it was for a person to be a life-long friend to another.

Yet in life, not everyone will desire to be life-long friends. For a lot of folks, when the going gets tough, they get gone. What I found to be true in my life is that, if you can have even a few devoted and faithful friends who will be by your side no matter what you're going through in life, then you can consider yourself most blessed.

Some people have a way with words when it comes to friendships, and that isn't always a good thing. You see, sometimes the words people may speak to you, even those you consider friends, are just words of hot air. I've had people whom I considered very close friends completely turn their backs and actually become angry with me over the fact I have gone deaf. It could be that perhaps at the time they were really more frustrated with the situation I was going through, but the end result was, that when I needed them most, they were least to be found. I was naïve and never anticipated such a thing would happen in the relationships I had at that point in my life. I guess it was time for me to experience the harsh reality that words are empty until filled with actions.

When I spoke at my mother's service, I reflected upon what it means to be a friend for life to another person. To be faithful and steadfast, regardless of what life may throw at you. It was with tears in my eyes and a huge lump in my throat I read the lyrics to that song. It helped me to be so grateful for the friendships I have with those whom I now know will be with me until I am in the hands of my Father in heaven.

I believe that God never closes a door without opening a window, and He most assuredly did this when it came to a few lost relationships, bringing into my life some new special friendships. One such relationship was brought about through an introduction by a very close friend of mine, Bob Taylor. Bob is the co-founder and president of Taylor Guitars. We've been great friends, like family, for over twenty-five years, and our families get together often for various BBQs and holidays. As I mentioned at the beginning of my book, Cindy Taylor, Bob's wife, has been my editor and champion to help me write and tell my story.

Now, the introduction that Bob brought about was to someone very special to him and Taylor Guitars. The guy is a master guitar player, an amazing musician and songwriter, and one of the most humble persons I've ever met. His name is Doyle Dykes. Bob introduced me to Doyle because he thought I could give some words of encouragement, as he was facing a similar surgery to remove an acoustic neuroma from his auditory nerve. Bob and Cindy were by my side the entire first brain surgery and watched me go deaf in my right ear. Bob and I were on the same worship team at our church for years and we loved playing music together. So, Bob truly felt I could bring some unique perspective to Doyle as a musician, as one having been through some of what he was facing.

Since that time, Doyle and I have developed a special friendship. We share a deep and special bond. Two guys who love God greatly, two guys who have a tremendous passion for music and creativity of song. Doyle is deaf in one ear and I'm totally deaf. It's great when we see each other; it's like the majority of our conversation falls on deaf ears ...

Another thing I admire about these two guys is that they both recently had their individual books published. Bob wrote his book *Guitar Lessons,*[5] which is all about Taylor Guitars and how he and his partner, Kurt, have built their business into being one of the leading guitar manufacturers in the world. Dolye's book, *The Lights of Marfa,*[6] is just one amazing story after another about his life, his music, and how God has been at work through both. I had been working on writing my story for over four years and in various formats, and before I knew it, two of my great friends had their books done. Both of these guys are such an inspiration to me. They are truly life-long friends to my family and me and have been a constant source encouragement for me to share my story with others.

There is another dear friend, without whom I most likely would not be writing this book. His name is Torrey Larsen, and we've been close friends for the past seventeen years. Although we can go months without connecting in person, our relationship is one of those in which, if time lapses without being able to get together for lunch, when we do finally meet up, we pick up right where we

---

5 Bob Taylor "Guitar Lessons" - A Life's Journey Turning Passion Into Business, Published by John Wiley & Sons, Inc. Hoboken, New Jersey 2011

6 Doyle Dykes "The Lights of Marfa" - One Of The World's Great Guitar Player's Amazing Encounters With God by Moody Publishers, Chicago, Il 2011

left off. Torrey has this wonderful demeanor, whereby he always makes me feel safe in being transparent about what's going on in my life. Some people refer to having someone like this in their life as having a personal confidant. Yet there is even more that he brings to my life. He is the type of friend who will tell you those things you hope to hear from someone you trust. The type of person who will share his words of encouragement and support, and who is willing to impart wisdom and suggestions in various life circumstances. Through some direct and loving words shared by this dear friend, I learned something of paramount importance during one of my life's most difficult times.

It had been a few months since Torrey and I had last been together, and we finally were meeting up at a local Mexican restaurant for lunch. I was at my lowest point in my life, where I was totally indifferent toward everything and everyone and just wanted to escape. During that lunch, Torrey asked me to make a pledge to him: that I would call him before I made any "damaging and harmful" choices. I use those words because I was hanging over the edge of the cliff of self-destruction, and Torrey knew I was close. When a friend makes you take an oath and promise that you'll call before you make a wrong turn in life, well, sometimes that's all a person needs. You see, I was never ready to make that call to him. I knew if I did, no matter what he had going on in life, he would have stopped everything and confronted me. He would have done all within his power to encourage me to not give up and to think through the impact my decisions would have upon those who loved me and would be most harmed.

One of the most important lessons I've learned in life about friendships through that experience is this: that a friend will often tell you what you want to hear, but a friend who truly cares the most about you, will tell you what you need to hear.

That day at lunch, I was hoping to walk away with words of encouragement and support, words I wanted to hear. Yet what I left with was a message of life-changing implications. I left with what I needed to hear from a friend. Someone who was not only willing to hold me accountable, but was willing to make himself available to help me fight the battles and challenges I faced.

Six years ago, I was venturing down the Highway to Hell and at a point of feeling as though I would never be able to completely trust another soul to be a true friend. Like I said earlier, God never closes a door without opening a window. In fact, I feel as though God has thrown open the window for me and blessed me with some truly wonderful people in my life. The kind I'd be willing to entrust my life to, people who I can honestly say that the remainder of my life won't be too long for us to be *friends.*

Patiently

I always thought the band Journey had such an amazing sound, much in part due to the iconic vocals of Steve Perry. I still hear his voice in my head when I read through the titles of songs they performed. It's hard to describe the emotions I feel, and have to battle, when the vivid memories of songs play back in my mind. On one hand, it's such a great blessing to recall literally hundreds of songs in such detail. On the other hand, it sometimes is more than I can deal with on any given day, and I just begin to well up with deep sadness to the point of tears as I try to face the reality of never being able to hear those songs again.

Yet in the daily struggles, with all the physical stuff and emotional battles, there is a peace I've come to know. It's not that it comes easy all of the time, but rather through times of having to be patient; waiting for the periods of anxiety, exhaustion, emotional and physical pain to subside, to reach the periods of deep peace that can only come from God.

Now, let me tell you with all truthfulness that I don't pretend to live in a constant state of peace. Because that's just not reality for me, and to convey anything close to that would just be void of integrity. Rarely does a day go by that I'm not struggling with one thing or another, and often with multiple issues at the same time. Frequently throughout the week, I will wake up at 4:30 or 5:00 in the morning from a sound sleep to the most horrific loud ringing, headaches, or dizziness you can imagine. Some days it takes hours before it begins to subside, while other days it never goes away until I fall back to sleep again that night. Days hold no certain pattern as various combinations of all these things come about with no precise warning. Stuff just happens and I have to do my best to deal with it.

I don't write this chapter with any intention of initiating some sort of theological or psychological debate. Quite frankly, I've learned that no one has the right to tell another person what they should feel or when they should feel it. Rather than try to tell you how you should feel, I'd prefer to focus on the *what,* so to speak. *What* I feel, *what* I believe, and *what* a difference it's made in my life.

Having read through my story thus far, you have undoubtedly discovered that I am a Christian in my faith. What does that mean specifically, you ask? Well, specifically, that means I believe Jesus Christ to be the Son of God and through His taking my sins upon Himself, dying on the cross and being raised from the grave three days later; that all my sins are and shall be forgiven and my name has been entered upon the pages of the book of eternal life. What feelings come over me as I think about that? Answer: peace.

What helps me get through each day? Answer: patience. The kind of patience that comes from trusting God in the moment and waiting *patiently* for His peace to be upon me. Some days it comes quickly, while other days it requires ongoing prayer throughout the day and meditating upon His promises found in His word, the Bible.

You see, one of the things I cling to as a follower of Christ is the fact that when I received Him as my Lord and thereby received God's gracious gift of salvation, I became a child of God and an heir to His kingdom. Simply put, one day I will be in His presence for all eternity and receive all of His promises. You might be asking, "So what? What difference does that make for you here and now, Tim?"

Well, it makes all the difference to me. Although I've been a Christian for most of my life, I never focused much on God's promises or eternity. When life was running smoothly and I still felt I had decades to live, I didn't give much thought about needing the promises of God. It's a lot like how people treat retirement planning in their early years. "We've got time and will get to that later in life." It's amazing how a crisis of faith and having your entire life disrupted can change your thinking. I remember coming across a quote: "When we're most uncertain about the immediate, we can be most certain about the ultimate." What a difference that concept has made in my life. Wow! I mean, with all the uncertainties in my life, I realized how much I needed to be certain of what ultimately was going to happen to me.

The very faith I profess in God through Jesus Christ is the foundation of the hope I now have each day. Hope in the promises from the Lord God Almighty Himself! You see, I came to be certain of the ultimate, that one day I'm gonna be hearing again and I'm going to be hearing the voices of multitudes of angels. One day, I'll be walking the streets of heaven, and it won't be with no stinking crutch or cane, either. There's going to come a time where there won't ever be another tear of sorrow, hurt, frustration, or despair falling from my eyes. There's gonna be a day where I'll never again be overcome with unbearable dizziness, severe headaches, ongoing facial spasms, or any other physical infirmities or emotional battles.

That's *what* makes me want to share my story! That's *what* motivates me to encourage others to believe in God and trust in Him! That's *what* inspires me to preach about God's mercies, grace, and goodness and of all His promises to those who will believe. That's *what* brings about a profound joy and peace within me and fills my heart with countless songs. That's *what* gets me through the day, each day, one day at a time, *patiently*!

Don't Stop Believin'

Sometimes, just when we think we've got a grasp on how to handle a situation, everything can head in the opposite direction. In life, we can be at a point where we are facing so many tough situations that the old adage seems to hold a viable truth: "when it rains, it pours." Hey, let me tell you, I can identify with that! Yet I believe wholeheartedly that's when our faith gets tested the most.

For some, the seasons of rain, those times of severe testing in life, are just too much to endure and they give up their trust and faith in God. My heart breaks when I see friends walk away from God, their marriages, children, and friends. Yet as one who was so close to that tipping point in life, I felt compelled to write the following to empathize with such circumstances and to encourage the reader to remain steadfast and faithful. Have I been through some storms in life? You bet! Right to the point where I didn't think I could keep on treading water.

You see, after I first found out about having a large brain tumor on my right side, the one I mentioned which was growing toward and was very close to my brainstem, my wife and I found out something equally as concerning. Neurofibromatosis type 2 is a genetic disorder. Simply put, it passes down from parent to child at a fifty percent probability rate for each child born.

It was such a heavy load for us to carry at that time. Here I was facing a life-threatening condition, a major brain surgery, and suddenly, my wife and I were confronted by the real possibility that one or both of our children could have this same disease. I remember how horrible and helpless I felt about knowing I may have passed something like this on to my children. They didn't do anything to possibly deserve this. I had such tremendous guilt, knowing that as their father, they may inherit this dreadful battle from me.

Well, we had our son tested not too long after my first surgery. The most effective way to determine if someone has NF2 is through a MRI scan, using contrast dye. It typically takes about a week to learn the results. When we finally heard back from the doctor, we discovered our son Dallas did, in fact, have NF2. It was one of the most difficult conversations we've ever had with him. He was only twelve years old at the time, and having seen what happened to me through my first surgery, needless to say, it was just an overwhelming situation for such a young guy to have to confront.

Our daughter Brittney was tested at the same time as Dallas, but there were no signs of her having this condition. She still could be at risk, even as I write this paragraph. She will need to be tested again at some point in the future, but both of our children, after witnessing all I've been through, are in no rush to try any type of experimental surgeries. They have also pretty much decided to opt out of any medical intervention unless they are facing a potentially life-threatening situation.

I can tell you, there are frequently still days that I carry a heavy burden for both our children. I then come back to the realization that my wife and I committed both of them into God's hands and His care, so no matter what, we both take great confidence that God is in control of this whole situation.

Both of them take all of this in tremendous stride. They both have an amazing outlook and show little concern for themselves, while focusing far more on what I go through. What a blessing they are to me on this journey.

One of the ironic aspects of all this is that our son Dallas is truly an amazing drummer. He plays with an absolute power-driven energy and is just flat-out entertaining to watch perform. His band, Hit Dog Hollar, just recorded and released their first CD entitled *Ruckus,* along with their first music video. I've been told all of their original music has a really hard Southern rock-style sound. Oh, man! How I wish I could hear them play. We've been to several of their concerts, and as much as I love watching them perform, it is always with some deep sadness accompanying the realization that I'll never be able to hear their music.

Yet, in the midst of this, I am so grateful I can watch them. I also love to see the reactions of friends and all those who come to see their shows. It just lights me up to see people diggin' their tunes and watching the show they put on.

Another aspect to all of this is the struggle I deal with on an emotional level trying to imagine what my children's voices sound like, as they are no longer in their teen years. That was their age when I went totally deaf, and they've both told me their voices have changed over the past seven years. It would have been a gradual transition and passed without a lot of thought when I had hearing. Now, I often think of it as I watch them converse, wondering if I'd recognize their voices.

Brittney used to sing her heart out to songs on the radio or CDs, and, like her mother, she has an unbelievable ability to memorize lyrics. I mean, we could be driving in the car and put in a new CD, and after about three or four times through, she already had most of the lyrics memorized. And this was back before she was a teenager. I loved hearing my baby girl sing. I would literally shake my head in amazement at how fast she could pick up songs and sing right along with the vocalists. I still often think she could have been a really good professional singer, but it wasn't something she wanted to pursue. Her heart is in helping others, and as I write this, she is working toward becoming a nurse and desires to work with children who have cancer. Yeah, I have to say, "I love her choice in pursuing a career where she can make a positive impact on the lives of little ones!"

There are so many aspects of daily life I could write about that relate to a father's heart toward his children and how much I feel I miss out on in not being able to hear them. Like I said before, it's a very different scenario when a person becomes completely deaf later in life than for someone who is born deaf or becomes so at an early age. You see, I know what I'm missing!

Another example of something I often think about is what it will be like when they are married. I often reflect upon the fact that I won't be able to hear them or their future spouses share their wedding vows. To imagine being there on one of the biggest days in their lives and not be able to hear them say "I do" is tough for me. I'm a big softy at heart, and like any dad who loves his children, I want to be a part of every significant aspect of their lives. I know I'll have someone there to type out all the words being said, but often things can get lost in translation. Not to mention that words on a computer screen miss the inflections and emotions of the voices, particularly in such an emotional setting as a wedding.

It's just part of life sometimes, how things work out so differently then we might have originally planned. Even down to those most basic things that I held in such confidence and never thought twice about. These unplanned experiences have cast me into a new perspective, changing the way I view so many aspects of life. I have a new awareness of many things in life I took for granted and didn't stop to fully appreciate or give thanks for.

I look forward to the years to come and all the future family activities I can possibly attend. God willing, I will be there for as many of Dallas' concerts as possible and visit Brittney wherever she is involved in making an impact on children's lives. I will be in front and (well, just a bit off) center at both their weddings and reading the lyrics of each song being performed and each word being expressed. I will be there when their children are born and eagerly wait for others to tell me what they sound like, and describe all of the noises their babies make. I will be there for my grandchildren, right by their sides with eyes wide open to behold all that awaits them. You see, I have great faith in God that I will get to witness all these things in my children's lives and that's what keeps me going in all this. Faith! My faith in Jesus Christ! And no matter what, I know I won't stop; and I continue to fervently pray that my family and dear friends likewise *don't stop believin'*.

Will It Go Round in Circles?

This was a great song by Billy Preston, and I used to listen to his songs all the time to learn how to establish grooves as a drummer. This song title is very descriptive of the overall direction in my life, which has seemingly come around in a full circle. As you read on here, you'll discover why.

Although I started out in music at the age of four, I don't remember music as being a part of my professional career desires until my senior year in high school. As a matter a fact, my first ambition going back to when I was between the ages of thirteen to fourteen was to become a preacher.

Prior to my family going to a Wesleyan denominational church when I was fourteen, we attended a progressive Catholic church in southeast San Diego. The name of the church was Christ the King, and it had a really great worship band with guitars, bass, and drums. Even though I was young, I was very much in tune with what was happening musically at that time. I remember how tight the bass player and drummer played together, and perhaps the reason for that was because of who the bass player was. You see, his name was Nathan East and, even back in those days, Nathan was playing the upright bass as well as the electric bass. Now in case you've never heard of Nathan East, well, let me tell you he's arguably one of the most recorded bass players in the music industry, not to mention someone who has toured with some of the top performers in the world.

But let me get back to my first true ambition in life: to become a preacher. You see, it was at Christ the King Church that I became an altar boy and wanted to be in ministry in some capacity. It was at this same time that I attended a Christian outreach program at San Diego State and I heard the amazing testimony of a former New York gang leader by the name of Nicky Cruz. His story had me glued to my seat, and I so vividly recall telling God I wanted to have a story like that to share with people. Yeah, I know what you're probably thinking: be careful what you ask for, because ... No, I didn't want to become a gang leader, but I wanted to impact people and have God get the glory for my story.

I became so focused on becoming a preacher that I applied to Oral Roberts University in Oklahoma. My freshman year in high school, I took a family vacation with my parents, and we drove across the country to see my mom's family. We actually went to ORU, visited the campus, and took a tour. It was such an impressive campus in those days (as I'm sure it still is today). I had a major all picked out, "music and youth ministry," and felt very confident in my musical abilities, grades, and letters of recommendation. I thought for sure this was going to be my future right after high school. Even my parents were one hundred percent supportive and were willing to pay for my education there, so we wouldn't be dependent upon scholarships for me to go to that school.

After about six months of waiting, I finally received my application results back from ORU, and was not accepted. At least not right after I was to graduate from high school. They had very limited space in those days as they had students attending from all over the world, and the letter they wrote encouraged me to leave my application on file with them and look into attending a junior college after high school. There were some other schools I thought about as well, but I decided I'd better get some college level classes under my belt and then apply to those schools.

Those few years remaining in high school sure passed quickly, and I had already been playing with some of San Diego's best performing bands. But my desire to become a preacher was still pretty strong, and so I attended Mesa Junior College in San Diego. Since music and youth ministries were still on the top of my list of college majors, I selected a couple of music classes and some other general education requirements. Although I was pushing forward, I must admit it wasn't with a lot of energy. I felt as though the wind had been let out of my sails after not going straight to a "big-time" college or university right after high school. I felt as though I was just going through the motions. But I was still moving forward, just not as I originally thought I would.

Now, watch how this worked out in my life (things coming around, the beginning of a circle). Just prior to the end of my first semester at Mesa Junior College, I got a call from a really popular show band. They had just returned from touring Japan and France and were back in the States getting ready for another tour. They had three front vocalists and a four-piece band and they put on an incredible show. They performed a lot of cover tunes as well as original songs and performed at large capacity show clubs. They always filled those clubs with overflowing crowds and the club owners loved them. This band had been on the road for nearly ten years and was really successful. I was eighteen at the time, and when they asked me to audition for the job, I was beyond excited. I thought, "This is it, my big break in the music industry. School can wait." I auditioned for them the day after they called me and I got the job. What was so amazing about this is that one of the guitar players in the band was Marcel East, brother of Nathan East.

Here it was some five years after I used to go to church and listen to Nathan as a bass player, and now I was about to go on tour with his younger brother, Marcel. Marcel was so talented and we connected right away as friends. Our first gigs were up in the state of Washington, and then we went to Vancouver, B.C. Shortly after, the band's managers weren't able to get immediate dates booked, and so we ended back in Federal Way, Washington to rehearse for future pending shows and recorded some songs in the studio. Like I said, I was eighteen at the time and I was missing my friends back home, and with no certain dates lined up, I decided to leave the band.

Within a few days of returning home, I was back with some of my friends from a previous band, and we were starting to build a new group with the former members of Higher Ground. One of the people we brought into the group for a short time was another awesome bass player from San Diego named Jason Scheff. Now, in case you don't recognize his name, let me point out why you've most likely heard his music and voice. Jason was one of the most talented musicians I ever worked with. We were in a few bands together, yet only played a couple of actual jobs as none of the groups got off the ground at that time. Jason could play several instruments and ended up in a local club band as their bass player. Later, Jason ended up becoming the bass player for the band Chicago—yeah, Chicago—and is still with them today.

As I mentioned in other chapters, my musical endeavors continued for many years after my high school days. There were lots of bands, a lot of hours in recording studios, most of which now seems like a blur. It was about fifteen years before I became deaf, that I went back to my roots of faith and decided to singularly focus on writing and performing Christian music. I did an album with my brother of songs we wrote together, and we did some local stuff around town in San Diego. As years passed, I became heavily involved playing on worship teams for my church, and it was there that Bob Taylor and I played in the same band for many years. It was such a great time for me. My whole thought process had come around full circle from where I was years earlier. God convicted me during that time that the only glory in life that will ever count are the works I do here and now for His glory.

As time passed, I became a worship leader of a very large Sunday school class at our church, averaging about one hundred eighty people per week in attendance. It was there I learned so much more about leading worship. Where once I was so driven by performance, showmanship, theatrics, and perfecting the mix of sound, I found myself having to learn some more painful truths about my life. You see, I got really wrapped up in the all those aspects of music—perfection, so to speak. I became so focused upon all those mechanics and components of musical performance that I lost sight of what matters most. God began to show me that I was more focused on the production of worship than the person of worship. I was looking at everything else involved instead of only looking toward the One I was there to worship in the first place.

It was at this time that I learned some very real truths about musical worship offered to God, and I'll point out just a few of these for you:

The first insight I gained was that worship is our gift back to God. It's the one thing He doesn't do for Himself.

Secondly, when I'm worshiping God, I shouldn't be doing it because of how it makes me feel. It has nothing to do with how I feel, but rather how it makes God feel. I worship God because it blesses Him.

So, the circle I talked about, where is it in all this? Well, remember I started this chapter by telling you about my first desire in what I wanted to become in life. That prior to ever thinking of becoming a professional musician, I wanted to become a preacher. Well, what I can tell you today without exception is that I no longer have any notions of being the best performing drummer in music, a worship leader, or business tycoon of sorts. It's all I can do each day to accomplish some basic household chores and to write a few e-mails, a few paragraphs in my journal, or prepare a Sunday school message. But look at that! The very thing I do now is just what I wanted to do in life from the very beginning. To share my story with others and to be of encouragement and a blessing to people who need to hear about God.

Will it go round in circles? Yeah, I think it will. In fact, I know it has and I am so thankful to God, for He's protected me and guided me full circle in life, by giving me the original desires of my heart.

Purple Haze

The 1960s brought about some amazing changes to secular music. It was a time of no absolutes, and one group after another began to develop their own unabashed sense of style to confront the issues of society. Freedom of speech allowed artists to pen lyrics with little reserve. Topics ranging from drug use and their effects (trips) all the way to pushing the envelope of the sexual revolution. "Free love," "love-ins," and protests against the war in Vietnam were making the daily headlines and the evening news.

I was a young child in the 60s, yet my musical tastes and record purchases were far beyond my years. I had all the current albums and listened to them until I literally had worn them out. Black light posters, hanging beads, and custom-painted walls adorned the bedroom my brother and I shared. My parents thought it was just a phase, but at that age, I believe much was engrained into my young, impressionable mind.

Looking back, and reflecting now as an adult, it is abundantly clear to me how society's pain was all too often being bandaged by unbridled personal pleasures. Sex, drugs, and rock 'n' roll were the cultural norm for so many, as teens and young adults were seeking escape through rebellious activity, discarding the values of older adults.

Call it a "purple haze," a cloud, or a dense fog thwarting clear thinking. We all have personal references to describe someone in this frame of mind. These words characterize a person with the inability to make clear decisions for their well-being and who thereby brings harmful or hurtful situations upon themselves and those around them.

My personal period of perpetual purple haze was detailed previously in the chapter "Stairway to Heaven or Highway to Hell." I was at such a dangerous place in life because I had "fallen asleep at the wheel" while trying to make my way through the obstacles I was facing. I admitted earlier I was numb in both feelings and thinking, and that I was heading toward becoming a person of moral indifference. I was on the verge of becoming blatantly careless in my thoughts and decisions, which would unequivocally lead to actions.

The tragedy of my being at that point in life and tolerating moral indifference is that my decisions and actions would impact more than just me. At that point in time, those around me were witness to me trying to push through the haze without sobriety of mind.

For some people, getting to this point occurs without any awareness. Life's circumstances can just mount an all-out attack with too many overwhelming challenges. I believe this is precisely what happened to me. I was totally caught off guard and woke up in the thick of things. You see, I allowed myself to become bored, frustrated, and discontented with life. I had positioned myself to become way too comfortable and digressed into a spiritual siesta. Call it fog, haze, or call it what you will, I was completely covered by its density, and that dampened all my fervor to follow my convictions. Back in 2006, I was trying to navigate on my own through a most dangerous situation, and there was no possibility for me to chart a course toward safety without the help of my wife and dearest friends.

It was without a doubt one of the most trying times for me. Let me say this: it wasn't easy for my wife or children, either. I have found that moral indifference can't live alongside spiritual convictions. What were once absolutes in my life became fuzzy, and my faith was shaken to its core. Suddenly, my faith was only as strong as what I could contemplate comfortably. I was only able to focus and think about that which was easiest to believe. What I know today is this: "that shallow thinking leads to shallow faith!"

Having driven hundreds of thousands of miles in my lifetime, I've encountered all types of dangerous weather conditions. From torrential rain, which forced me to seek cover under a freeway underpass, to severe winds and tornado warnings through the very areas I was driving. Then there was the fog ... the most incredibly dense fog you can imagine. I was on the highway with a posted speed limit of sixty-five miles per hour and I was only able to drive at twenty miles per hour. I couldn't see a single car length in front of me, and I drove for a good while like that until I found a truck stop to park and wait until the fog lifted. Sometimes it's best to pull off the road and wait until the imminent dangers have passed by. To seek cover from the severe situation and sit and talk with some people who can assure you that you're not the only one going through diverse and dangerous circumstances in life.

As I write these words, I can tell you without hesitation that I am forever indebted to those who were so gracious and demonstrated both their compassion and their long-suffering toward me! Their willingness to be patient with me and endure the process of my journey is what now enables me the opportunity to encourage others who are in the midst of such adversity, or are facing it with a friend or loved one. If I could impart a single thought of inspiration for those on a similar journey through their own *purple haze,* I would say to you, "Stay the course! Don't give up! Let me assure you, the fog will lift and the storm will pass. Head for the shelter of those who love you most and seek their comfort, protection, and prayers. The journey, however difficult, is one worth traveling when you put your trust and faith in God!"

Ain't No Mountain High Enough

This was one of the all-time great R&B songs. Written by Nickolas Ashford and Valerie Simpson and originally recorded by Marvin Gaye and Tammi Terrell, it was a megahit. It's been re-recorded numerous times over the years. It's a song I grew up with, and when Diana Ross recorded and released the song, it became a solo number one hit on Billboard and was nominated for a Grammy Award in the early 70s.

When I was writing the closing chapters of this book, I reflected a great deal about what to write for my concluding thoughts. I never intended to share my story from a standpoint of "woe is me," thereby creating the default questions of, "Why do such tragic and challenging things happen to decent people?" The truth is, I hope that in reading my story, you've come to appreciate the blessings in life. You know, all the little things we take for granted on a daily basis, the simple things, so to speak. When I speak at churches or in a Sunday school class, the goal in sharing my testimony is for people to hear the power of God's unfailing love, mercy, and compassion. Even in the midst of the most difficult of times, God is faithful!

As I was thinking about all kinds of song titles to use near the end of my writing this book, I was praying one day and just asked God to give me a song. What's odd is this ain't no spiritual hymn or a song found in the gospel arena. It's a secular tune with a message about the love of someone who is committed; their vow to the other person is, nothing will separate the love they have for the other. The message is clear that there's no distance or any obstacle, which would be too high or low enough to diminish that love.

In the midst of singing the melody and lyrics in my head, I suddenly found myself recalling one of God's great promises to me. Now, if I get a little preachy here, it's because I don't want to mess up the truth. You see, I think the lyrics of the very song "Ain't No Mountain High Enough" might have been inspired right from the very same promise found in the Bible.

Now, before I share the passage of these words with you, "the promise," I need to provide you with a brief background of the person who wrote these words. His name was Paul, and he wrote much of the New Testament in the Bible. When I take even a brief look into his life's testimony, reading what he endured, I find myself all the more passionate about the promise of God, given to Paul to write down for each of us. Paul endured more than most of us could ever comprehend. Consider these words, which he wrote:

> *I've worked much harder, been jailed more often, beaten up more times than I can count, and at death's door time after time. I've been flogged five times with the Jews' thirty-nine lashes, beaten by Roman rods three times, pummeled with rocks once. I've been shipwrecked three times, and immersed in the open sea for a night and a day. In hard traveling year in and year out, I've had to ford rivers, fend off robbers, struggle*

with friends, struggle with foes. I've been at risk in the city, at risk in the country, endangered by desert sun and sea storm, and betrayed by those I thought were my brothers. I've known drudgery and hard labor, many a long and lonely night without sleep, many a missed meal, blasted by the cold, naked to the weather. THE MESSAGE (2 Corinthians 11:23–27)

Come on now. When you read just those few brief accounts, you can just tell that Paul had been through the ordeals of life. Yet look at what he writes in regard to God's love and faithfulness through Jesus Christ:

So, what do you think? With God on our side like this, how can we lose? If God didn't hesitate to put everything on the line for us, embracing our condition and exposing himself to the worst by sending his own Son, is there anything else he wouldn't gladly and freely do for us? And who would dare tangle with God by messing with one of God's chosen? Who would dare even to point a finger? The One who died for us—who was raised to life for us!—is in the presence of God at this very moment sticking up for us. Do you think anyone is going to be able to drive a wedge between us and Christ's love for us? There is no way! Not trouble, not hard times, not hatred, not hunger, not homelessness, not bullying threats, not backstabbing, not even the worst sins listed in Scripture ... None of this fazes us because Jesus loves us. I'm absolutely convinced that nothing—nothing living or dead, angelic or demonic, today or tomorrow, high or low, thinkable or unthinkable—absolutely nothing can get between us and God's love because of the way that Jesus our Master has embraced us. THE MESSAGE (Romans 8:31–39)

That's it! That's what I want to leave you with and challenge you to consider as the ultimate hope for you to embrace. People ask me all the time, "Tim, how do you do it? How do you get through all of this and keep positive and want to inspire others? Why aren't you angry? How come you're not mad at God for letting this happen to you?"

Well, read the words above one more time, and if you don't get it, read them again ... and again if need be. The truth is, you can't escape God's love once you give your life to Him. I tried to run from Him, tried to hide, tried to bury myself in indulgences to mask the ongoing physical and emotional stuff. But you know what? I had to find out for myself, when I was at the end of my rope, the very bottom of the pit and lost in life, that God's love for me was greater than everything I was facing. God is bigger than my issues, fears, and troubles.

As I write these words, I realize there's no way to tell my story without having written this chapter. Without God, there is no story of my life worth writing. There is neither message nor hope to be found unless it's conveyed to you as I've experienced it and am living it each day, even at this very moment.

What I've discovered again in life is that God's love for me surpasses everything else. What I found to be true in what Paul wrote about, as he penned onto paper words inspired by God, was this relevant truth and a great promise:

There is nothing – no space, time or dimension – that can keep me nor separate me from God's love. God loves me! He loves you! He wants you to enjoy a personal relationship with Him and experience that specific kind of love. The inseparable, unconditional, limitless love He has for you.

Music will always be a part of who I am, and the songs of my heart are the notes inspired by God as a result of His love and faithfulness. These songs are the melodies that have helped me to navigate through life's most challenging circumstances. As God continues to unfold His symphony of my life, I find great peace and strength in knowing He is the one whom I can depend upon through all situations. I believe that the greatest journey we will ever embark upon is the one that leads us home. For me, as I travel from a world of silence toward pursuit of living an abundant life, I purpose to do so with steadfast confidence. I know that God will lead me every step of the way on this most amazing adventure, as I journey from deaf to life.

Prayer for You

It would be difficult at best to detail how many songs have included references in their lyrics of "praying for you" in one form or another. Most are written with a heart of sincerity, with personal reflections and requests being offered up for that person. Some of the words are greatly specific and leave little room for speculation or interpretation of their intent or whether they are petitioning God. Other such lyrics, on the other hand, are vague at best, leaving the listener (or reader) to try to discover the truth of the author's message.

While working through the editing process, it became apparent to me that perhaps there would be someone who would read the preceding chapters and desire to know more about how to know God. Someone who would desire to know that his or her eternal destination would be certain—even more so for those who are most uncertain at this very moment.

And so, as I close with these final words, I do so in writing a *prayer for you,* one which you can pray out loud or in the quiet of your heart. No matter, God will hear you and He will be faithful to answer.

Lord Jesus, I need you. I ask you to come into my life and into my heart. I confess that I'm in need of a savior and I believe, in fact, that you did come to Earth to reconcile my life back into a relationship with you. I believe that you took upon yourself the sins of the world, which included my sins. Having done so, you faced the cross and gave your life willingly upon that cross so that my sins would be forgiven and that I could be justified and found not guilty before God in Heaven. I believe that you were buried and three days later arose from the grave having conquered death, and that one day, I will be with you in heaven. I ask for you to guide me and lead me; make me the kind of person you would have me become. Thank you, Lord God, for loving me so and for hearing my words. I pray this in the name of Jesus Christ. Amen!

Perhaps that which I've written has meant more to you than just reading mere words and you've felt a stirring within your heart. It may be that what you've just read was truly a prayer and that you've asked Christ to become Lord of your life. For others, it may be that you have been a believer in Christ yet have gotten off the road, have deviated down a different direction in life, and have distanced yourself from God. If either scenario is applicable to you at this precise moment in time, then I want to encourage you to seek out other believers in Christ. Look for a local church to get connected. A church that is a good Bible-teaching church that teaches that salvation can only come from the Lord Jesus Christ and by faith alone.

With my final words in writing this book, I leave you with a thought I'm paraphrasing from Henry Ward Beecher. He would often share that there are two classifications of people in this world, "the whosoever wills and the whosoever won'ts." Simply put, you'll either be joining Jesus Christ in His kingdom and be with Him in heaven for all eternity or you won't. God leaves the decision up to us. My only question for you is, what will you do with the Lord Jesus Christ, the living Son of God?

Afterword: Timothy's Mission

The name Timothy in Greek means "honoring God." It is from this translation, to honor God, that my heart has become so greatly inspired to share my story and the gospel of Christ Jesus. In my innermost being, at the core fiber of my soul, my utmost passion is to bring a message of hope, a testimony of God's unfailing faithfulness and unconditional love for all who will receive Jesus, His Son.

When Paul wrote the following words to Timothy, his dear friend and helper in ministry, he was writing to encourage him and clarify his role as pastor to the church at Ephesus. He wrote these words in the last days prior to his death. His time was coming to an end, and he was well aware of the urgency to set forth his personal desires and inspired words from the Holy Spirit.

It was his charge, command, and plea to young Timothy to remain faithful and eager to serve God, through all situations and circumstances. His words to Timothy remain as inspiring for us today as they did nearly two thousand years ago. They are full of urgency for us to share the gospel with as much dedication and fervor as he so commissioned this young man, who was a faithful servant and minister before the Lord.

> *I can't impress this on you too strongly. God is looking over your shoulder. Christ himself is the Judge, with the final say on everyone, living and dead. He is about to break into the open with his rule, so proclaim the Message with intensity; keep on your watch. Challenge, warn, and urge your people. Don't ever quit. Just keep it simple. You're going to find that there will be times when people will have no stomach for solid teaching, but will fill up on spiritual junk food—catchy opinions that tickle their fancy. They'll turn their backs on truth and chase mirages. But you—keep your eye on what you're doing; accept the hard times along with the good; keep the Message alive; do a thorough job as God's servant.*
>
> *THE MESSAGE* (1 Timothy 4:1–5)

The words from this exact passage were shared during my formal induction as a Bible teacher and minister of God's word. They have become my personal core statement of charge and accountability. As a result, all proceeds from sales of this book will go towards furthering the gospel and building up the body of Christ Jesus. With both focused purpose and tremendous passion, it is my earnest commitment to further preach the gospel and share my testimony of God's faithfulness. In the event you would like to purchase additional copies of this book, you can do so online through **Family Discipleship Ministries**:

www.familydiscipleshipministries.org

I would love the opportunity to share my testimony at your church or special event. To inquire about scheduling dates or information: www.timothysmission.org

For personal correspondence: timmauricio7@gmail.com

CPSIA information can be obtained
at www.ICGtesting.com
Printed in the USA
LVHW090817100320
649520LV00001B/3

9 780990 335030